Bringing Harmony by Ha

Bringing Harr
Ops Warriors I
Book Two

by Harley McRide

© Copyright July 2014 JK Publishing, Inc.
All cover art and logo © Copyright July 2014 by JK Publishing, Inc.
All rights reserved.

Edited by Caroline Kirby
Artwork by Jess Buffett
Published by JK Publishing, Inc.

JK Publishing, Inc.

Smashwords Edition, License Notes

This eBook is licensed for your personal enjoyment only. This eBook may not be re-sold or given away to other people. If you would like to share this book with another person, please purchase an additional copy for each recipient. If you are reading this book and did not purchase it or it was not purchased for your use only, then please return to Smashwords.com, and purchase your own copy.

Thank you for respecting the hard work of this author.

This is a work of fiction. Names, places, characters and incidents either are the product of the author's imagination or are used fictitiously and any resemblance to any actual persons, living or dead, organizations, events or locales are entirely coincidental.

No part of this book may be reproduced, stored in a retrieval system, or transmitted by any means without the written permission of the author and publishing company.

Piracy

Please always be aware of where you are purchasing your electronic books and from whom. Only purchase from reputable, licensed individuals such as Amazon, Barnes & Noble, iTunes, etc. If ever in doubt, let the author know of a suspected site illegally selling their works—remember to include a link to the site where you have found a book you suspect of being pirated. It only takes a moment of your time, but you will forever have the gratitude of an author.

About the eBook Purchased

Your purchase of this eBook allows you to only ONE LEGAL copy for your own personal reading on your own personal computer or device. You do not have resale or distribution rights without the prior written permission of both the publisher and the copyright owner of this eBook. This eBook cannot be copied in any format, sold, or otherwise transferred from your computer to another through upload to a file sharing peer-to-peer program, free or for a fee, or as a prize in any contest. Such action is illegal and in violation of the U.S. Copyright Law. Distribution of this eBook, in whole or in part, online, offline, in print or in any way or any other method currently known or yet to be invented, is forbidden. If you do not want this eBook anymore, you must delete it from your computer.

    WARNING: The unauthorized reproduction or distribution of this copyrighted work is illegal. Criminal copyright infringement, including infringement without monetary gain, is investigated by the FBI and is punishable by up to 5 years in federal prison and a fine of $250,000.

    If you find any e-books being sold or shared illegally, please contact the author or the publishing company.
    Email: jkpublishing@jkpublishingbooks.com

Dedication

I never thought in a million years that I would actually have fans, and great ones at that. I love the group we have developed on Facebook, and so many wonderful people are in there because they love the MC world. So this is for my fans, and the people in my group on Facebook. Especially, Mary Orr, who has been a godsend for me in the group, your efforts are appreciated!

Visit me at my Facebook page: https://www.facebook.com/harley.mcride?fref=ts

I would love to hear from you.

Table of Contents

Dedication
Prologue
Chapter One
Chapter Two
Chapter Three
Chapter Four
Chapter Five
Chapter Six
Chapter Seven
Chapter Eight
Chapter Nine
Chapter Ten
Chapter Eleven
Chapter Twelve
Chapter Thirteen
Chapter Fourteen
Chapter Fifteen
Chapter Sixteen
Chapter Seventeen
Epilogue
Books by Harley McRide
Excerpt from Bed of Roses
Excerpt from Big Dog

Prologue

Harmony stepped into the main room of the Ops Warriors main building. The room was packed, but she knew everyone. Smiling and waving, she went in search of the two men who she had been dreaming of for the last six years. She had offered her company's services to the club, and she had been waiting for them to have church. Harmony thought she had proved herself when they had thrown her a case for one of the members. They had to look at her as an adult now.

Shady was laughing and holding a beer when she approached her friend. The woman was a legend in the MC world. A woman being a member of an MC was unusual, but she had earned her status a few years ago when there was an incident at the mine. No one knew for sure what happened other than Shady had been by herself and called for the cleaners late one night. She had been bloodied and bruised when she came back to the compound. Harmony and her best friend, Lyla, were called because Shady had only wanted to have her help her get cleaned up. They were the only two people besides the men who knew exactly what happened. It made her shiver to think of that night, and her friend had changed a lot after that night. Harmony had grown up a lot since that night as well.

She knew what it was like to live in an MC group; they were a family first and foremost. They also had strict rules on certain things. Messing with the child of a member was one of the biggest rules you could break. You had to have permission, Harmony knew it, but she also knew she loved those two men. Some people may not understand it, and she didn't care. She grew up watching people fall in love and none of it was normal, it was messy, heartbreaking, and most of all beautiful. Who cared if she loved two men, they would take care of her.

"Hey, girl," Shady said and smiled at her. "You are looking good tonight. I assume it is 'cause Fish is busy." She was like an older sister to her, and she was also well aware of the feelings she had for Creed and Fork.

"Shut up," Harmony laughed. "I can dress how I want, just turned twenty-two you know, so I am pretty sure my dad doesn't have a say in what I wear."

"Right, keep living that dream." Shady laughed and pulled a beer from behind the bar and handed it to her.

Harmony's birthday had been two months ago, she had refused a party her dad was going to throw her because the people she wanted there would not have shown up. Tonight she was going to show them how grownup and ready she was.

She stood and talked with Shady and some of the girls who came up to talk to them. Most of them were the club whores, and she ignored them. The others, the girls who lived in the compound and were strippers at Bitches, she liked; of course it was because most of them who lived there had a past and needed a family connection like she did. Plus, they weren't like the whores; they strictly belonged to the Ops Warriors.

Harmony wasn't stupid, she knew what went on at these parties, but she also knew that if anyone of these men found the love and acceptance they were all looking for they would be faithful. She planned to show them just that.

The party roared on around her and she remained in the position leaning up against the bar waiting, they would put in an appearance soon, they had to. Harmony laughed and greeted most of the club as she stood there, all of them commenting on how good she looked. It made her confidence rise to the point she convinced herself there was no way they could ignore her. Finally, three hours and five beers later, the two men of her dreams came into the room. That was when she learned what heartbreak really felt like.

They skimmed over the people, smiling and laughing. She knew they knew about her feelings toward them, she hadn't been shy about expressing her attraction, but they had just ignored it. No more, she thought and pushed herself away from the bar and began to thread her way through the people to get to their side.

She was short, she knew it and most of the time it didn't bug her unless there were people standing in her way, like they were right now. Most of the time people didn't even notice her trying to move around them. So when she finally drew near them, they didn't notice her. She had overshot them as they were standing in a circle of men, all of the leaders of the Ops Warriors MC.

When she heard her name she paused, Kink was talking about her. "Harmony came in a few hours ago, she has been drinking too, man. Think we should call Fish? We need to get this shit done before it gets out of hand, tonight was supposed to be a celebration, beginning of some new shit."

Creed made a noise of impatience. "Damn it, I told Fish to keep her away from the clubhouse tonight. How much has she had?"

"About five," Kink said and then Fork said something. There was another comment but she couldn't hear, but if they said her father's name, then they were talking about her, she was the only daughter of Fish. Fork argued then.

"Man, we are gonna have to do something about her now, Harmony being here forced our hand, we can't have her coming in here and partying tonight." There was a loud cheer and she lost track for a second of what they were saying. "Some of the guys from the other clubs are gonna think she is free and clear, open for business. This fucking shit is getting out of control, man; you would think we gave her a ring or something. Harmony will not understand this shit."

"We are going until we talked to everyone, things are going to change around here, fuck, we are going to have to talk to him again. Bitch does not know her place. Her little side project isn't going to be in this club, man. We have too much on the line to let that shit come in here. We gave her a one time deal, fucking stay away, I figured she would back off," Creed said. "She just keeps showing up. I know he told her too, I don't know why she is being so thick."

Harmony sucked in a breath; they didn't think she belonged here? She was an annoyance? No way did she just hear that. If nothing else, her company was solid, she had done things right, even her professors said she was going to be a kickass investigator.

"Shady and the girls need to cut her loose, she will keep doing this, and coming around as long as the girls don't say anything."

Poke snorted. "Man, you guys are pussies. You know she is only here because she is trying to lay claim you two, be man enough to turn her down and get on with it. It's not like you are ever gonna tap that. She will get bored with the business she has, not like it is gonna go anywhere; just tell her the truth, man. We aren't doing her any favors by lying to her. She is not club material, and she never will be."

Easy laughed. "Yeah, you got your sights set on some sweet ass. You had better hope Fish doesn't kill you before you get laid, man. He isn't going to like coming to collect her ass, shit, he was planning on talking to Harmony tomorrow."

How dare they talk about her like that? Harmony fumed, but then her heart was crushed when she heard Creed say.

"Yeah, one of you guys get Shady over here, we need to cut her loose now, this shit is not going to fly. Too much going on, she has been taking too many things for granted, bringing her business into the club uninvited, she needs to hear now, no more. She is not club material, and she will never be club material. Besides, I am sick of fucking avoiding the floor when she is here, we had plans for tonight, had to change shit until later," Creed laughed.

Harmony froze—they knew and had been avoiding her? How humiliating. They didn't want her. Well that was fine. Turning on her heel, she left the party without talking to anyone. By the time she reached the small house her and her father shared on the compound grounds she had been furious and embarrassed.

As she walked in, her father had been worried about the tears that were flowing down her face. The following days she refused to go with her father when he went to the compound for meetings or picnics like she had in the past.

Finally, she got it, and she wasn't going to forget it. They didn't want her, she was wasting no more time on Creed and Fork, they could fuck off.

Chapter One

Two years later...

"Who the fuck is buzzing the front gate?" Creed yelled into the darkness. The party had barely ended just before sunrise. Creed's head had only hit the pillow a few seconds ago when he heard the buzz on his phone.

Fuck, he thought and rose from the bed still clad in a pair of jeans. Not bothering to grab a shirt, he picked up the phone and looked down. Easy and Poke had the cameras to the front streamed through their phones so they could see if something was going on.

His eyes narrowed at the Prospect who was on guard duty and the tiny little woman who was arguing with him. *Not possible*, he thought. She would never have come here unless something was wrong.

"Let her in," he ordered into his phone and the Prospect jumped and nodded. He saw the smirk cross the woman's face as she walked onto the property. *She had a bit of a walk*, Creed mused, *and maybe the courtesy of letting her in would tame her attitude. Nah, he would never be so lucky.*

Creed walked down the stairs, opened the front door, and waited. He looked over the mess in the common room and shrugged, she'd seen worse, he was sure. He turned as he heard the footsteps on the gravel. He took her in, from her strawberry blonde hair, tight little body, and the green eyes that were currently cutting right through him. She was beautiful.

"What the fuck?" Creed growled at the woman who stood before him with her arms crossed.

"Don't you 'what the fuck' me, asshole. Your fucking bullshit war has bled over into my life. You need to fix this shit and fix it now before I shoot you myself," the woman said.

Yep, knew I couldn't be so lucky.

"Harmony," Creed sighed and shook his head.

"No, not going there," the little spitfire said and walked closer to him pointing her finger. "Dad said this was going to be possible, POSSIBLE, and yet here I am because it fucking happened. You know I should never have accepted this case."

"And yet you did." Creed smirked.

"Because my *father* asked me to, not you. I told you a year ago, I was *not* going to be cleaning up anymore of your messes and I am not. However, for some reason dad seems to like the woman, Freedom," Harmony barked and then her eyes narrowed. "Oh look, can't speak to Mutt without Jeff coming along. Fork, don't bother coming out and trying to smooth shit over. Thanks to your shit, our offices were on the receiving end of five Molotov cocktails last night. Just left the police station, they think it's the Diablos. So I came out here to tell you that dad and I are off the case. I am not getting pulled back into this shit again just 'cause you dipshits can't contain your fights."

"Creed," Fork said with a hard tone and he put his head down. Damn it, they knew something like this could happen, but seriously, they thought they had a little bit of time to contain this shit. After what happened to Free, and then the shit going down with the Devil Savages, everything was getting fucked up.

"Harmony," Creed tried again. "Come inside, where is Fish?"

"Since he is the DA, and he hired my firm to deal with the investigation into the Diablos, he is taking this as a threat against the office. *So*, he is making plans to keep everyone there safe, including Freedom," Harmony said sarcastically. "But I kinda felt like I should lay the blame on where it was needed—you dipshits."

"Well at least that hasn't changed." Fork laughed and shook his head.

"What?" She frowned.

"Your attitude," Fork smiled and rocked back on his feet. "Was getting a little boring around here without your mouth, Shady will be happy to see you're back."

"I am not back," she ground out.

"Oh you are back," Creed said and bent over, picked her up and threw her over his shoulder carrying her into the clubhouse.

*****

Harmony sat with her arms folded glaring at the two men who were at their desks in the main office area of the compound. There were a lot of desks in there now, where before there had only been one, Creed's. Harmony hadn't been there in two years and apparently, things had changed. Of course, back then, the club had been buying up businesses right and left.

Looking around while refusing to make eye contact with the guys, she took everything in. Growing up with her father, she knew what the MC club did, and she didn't care. One of the things she had to learn growing up, the line could be crossed, if it was for the greater good. Her father had been in the military for twenty years, they paid for his college to become a lawyer, and when he got out, he became the DA for the town. But he had always loved his bike, and when the Ops Warriors changed hands to Creed and his bunch, he became active in the club again.

Not that he hadn't been active before, he had been when he was in the military and stationed there. But when he became the DA, Fish had drawn the line and Creed's father, Limbo, had respected it. Her father still was a biker at heart, but of course, some of the activities the club was involved in wouldn't look good on a resume. So, the club and her father agreed to disagree on some things. Harmony couldn't just distance herself from the only family she knew, leaving her father to accept it grudgingly.

Fish was a single father, her mother decided the day Harmony was born she was not meant to be a mother, and she signed over her parental rights and left the hospital and her father alone with a newborn. The guys at the club had picked up the slack and been there for her father. That was how she had grown up, with some of the meanest badasses in the country. That being said, she also had grown up with a distinct impression on white, black, and grey areas of the world. She also respected that her father lived in a grey area.

When she was old enough to understand, Harmony realized her father wouldn't turn a blind eye if one of the guys got caught doing something illegal; however, he also didn't seek out reasons to bust them. Limbo knew this and worked his magic on the local police so he had protection. The club did things for the community and they were known for keeping the town safe. Therefore, the townspeople overlooked the club's illegal activities.

Harmony met Creed and Fork when her dad brought her to a picnic just after he had gotten out of the military. She had fallen in love with them at first sight; of course, she had been a young teen then, with stars in her eyes. For years she followed them around, became their shadow, and they let her. Creed had grown up in the club the same as her, but she had never known him because her dad kept her away from the club until she was old enough to understand what they were about. She knew the guys who helped raise her were into motorcycles but that was about it. Once Fish brought her to a family party though, and she saw Creed and Fork, two enlisted men who were like heroes to everyone in town, Harmony had decided right then and there they were hers. It wasn't until she was twenty, and she let her interest in the two men be known, that they had a problem.

Two men, it would usually freak most people out, but then most people didn't grow up in a motorcycle club. She learned and was taught that love was love, you didn't fuck around with it. Who cared if you loved one man, or two men. As long as they were loyal and understood club life, who cared? She had seen several ménage relationships and they had all been loving. So when she saw two men who without a shadow of a doubt were her dream men, she didn't blink—she just waited.

The sad part, was that through the years she saw the women they were attracted to. It was heartbreaking but Harmony convinced her young heart they hadn't seen her yet. When she found out they actually had, and just chose to ignore her, it crushed her.

She had graduated from college with a degree in Criminal Justice, no, she had no desire to be a police officer, besides, Harmony didn't take orders from people very well. So, her father suggested opening her own private investigation firm. She jumped on the idea and never looked back; being young and inexperienced, she hired one of the guys from the club who used to be Security Forces in the military. Monk was like a second father to her, and gave her firm credibility. At twenty-two, most people laughed when they saw she was the CEO. So Monk became the face of Hill Investigations, and the club had been their first client.

Creed and Fork had taken over from Limbo a few years previous, and she had watched them turn the club in a new direction. Her father approved of it, because certain things like running drugs were things of the past. The club was basically legitimate, all except for their guns, that was acceptable because the guns were supplied to many underground agencies that helped abused women get away from their abusers.

Harmony liked this about the club and was more than happy to help with it. However, they didn't think she could deal with it until Monk came into the fold. Then they were all over it. Over the last few years when Harmony had refused to have anything to do with the club socially, she had still made sure she helped the agencies that needed it. This is what made her so successful so fast, because Harmony and Monk had no tolerance for abuse and they would do whatever it took to get women out of a bad situation—anything.

She had been thrilled to work with the guys, knowing that once they saw her as a grownup now, they couldn't help but want her. She had been so wrong, and humiliated too. It had been awful, the night she had planned to give them her virginity, and her love. It had been the night of a party for some kind of announcement the next day. Harmony had dressed with care, wearing a classic little black dress she knew she looked good in.

Her father wasn't going to the party because he was taking depositions that night so she knew she was in the clear. Everything had been set, but when she walked into the party and searched for the men who had stolen her heart, she had been devastated...

Now here she was, two years later, right where she did not want to be, back in this godforsaken compound and they were suddenly interested in her life.

Creed folded his arms over his chest and looked at Harmony, she felt like a fucking bug under a microscope. The silence in the room was nerve racking, but she knew what they were doing. Fucking Alpha men who thought they could scare her. *Fuck that*, grinning, Harmony uncrossed the arms over her chest and met their eyes with a bored expression. She wanted to grin when both men cursed and shook their heads.

"Harmony, why don't you tell us why you decided to come here." Creed sighed.

"Why? Let me think, um, your fucking club is in danger you prick. I am pretty sure you know exactly who threw the fucking Molotov cocktails in my office. And who the fuck does that these days, I mean, those were so twenty years ago, shit, now you can get your hand on a bomb and just blow shit up. But nooooo, I am stuck with the assholes who leave a mess, at least if they would have blown up my office it would be cleaner, well for me," Harmony grumbled and both men were staring at her like she was nuts.

"Are you kidding me right now? What was Fish thinking? Why the fuck did he put you on this case?" Creed bellowed and Harmony sat straight up in her chair.

"You had better think before you speak one more word, asshole," Harmony yelled and Fork stepped between the two and held up his hand with a grin.

"Let's settle down for a second here," the VP said and Harmony glared at him.

"No, Spoon, let's not settle down, let's get this shit out in the open," Harmony said.

Fork frowned and turned to Harmony and said, "It's Fork and you damn well know it."

Harmony laughed. She knew how he got his name; they all knew how he got his name. While at dinner one night, a rival gang had started shit with them, Fork had been quick and grabbed the fork he was eating with and stabbed the man in the hand before things got completely out of hand. It had made the point with the other men who were hassling them and the situation had gone down as one of the funniest in club history.

"Do I?" Harmony snapped.

"You can't stab someone in the hand with a spoon," Fork snapped back and Harmony laughed and shook her head.

"Whatever, Spoon, now hear this," Harmony said. "I am good at my job, have developed a good reputation, and no one is going to tell me how the hell to run it."

"Woman, you are still wet behind the ears," Creed snarled. "Just seeing the clusterfuck this is shows how sloppy you have been. They never should have been able to find out you were investigating them."

Harmony rolled her eyes and then said, "They knew because I went right to the source and asked the leader of the Diablos a few questions. The two shits who are being held for Freedom's kidnapping were refusing to help, and we needed some answers. Put them on notice they are not bulletproof."

Creed and Fork stepped back and stared at her once again like she had lost her mind.

"You went into the Diablos crib and questioned him by yourself? Harmony, that was stupid, it put you on the map," Creed said, running his hand through his hair and messing it up. She loved it when he did that, made him look like he just woke up. Something Harmony had wanted to see a few years ago, now it made her want to grab a pair of clippers and go to town.

"Of course I didn't, geeze, I am not an idiot. I actually did graduate with a degree, and know how to protect myself. For your information, my office handles the investigations for not only the town, but several more. Monk and I have been making a name for ourselves," Harmony said.

"Yeah, we have heard," Creed said and stepped closer. "But Monk is the one who runs things."

"Are you kidding me, have you even talked to him about it, 'cause I can guarantee he is not saying that. He helps out, he is the face of the company because I am young, but make no mistake, I am the boss of Hill Investigations," Harmony yelled and both Creed and Fork frowned and looked at each other. Yeah, they hadn't bothered to ask, they only saw and thought what they wanted to and that pissed her the fuck off.

When they would have asked more questions, Harmony held up her hand. "Whatever, I don't have time for this, I came to tell you the shit you are pulling is bleeding over, so you need to step back. My dad is going to make sure they go down."

"You don't even know the half of it," Creed said and Fork got stiff. The Diablos weren't just messing with them, they were also messing with another club they had ties to. Fork made a noise of disgust.

"Devil Savages," Fork ground out. "Look into it."

"Wait," Creed said. "She is *not* looking into anything."

"Yes, I am," Harmony said and then stepped forward. "In fact, I need to get back to town. Fish and Monk are probably waiting for me."

"They can come out here," Creed said firmly.

"No, I will go there." Harmony laughed and went to walk out the door when she was pulled back and put in a chair, her wrist was handcuffed to the desk she had been sitting in front of before she could even take a breath. "What the fuck?" she yelled loudly.

"They can come out here," Creed said and sat down while she yelled and grabbed his cell. Fork shook his head and smiled.

Yeah, Harmony was back.

Chapter Two

Creed and Fork knew they were going to be in for a battle, something had happened two years ago to make Harmony stop coming to the club. They both knew it was bad because Harmony had been hanging around the club for years, but they didn't know what. Not that it had been a bad thing, she was the daughter of one of the old timers, and at the time there had been too many new guys coming and going. Creed and Fork had just realized they wanted her, both of them. They had started thinking that for the first time when she was twenty but gave her time to grow up.

Seeing her after so long, Creed hadn't been able to believe his eyes. She had grown up in two years, lost her baby face, and turned into a gorgeous young woman. Fork agreed, he could tell the way he was looking at her. Later they were going to have to talk. But after seeing her, he wasn't letting her take the risks she had been. It was crazy, Freedom had almost died because of those bastards, and Harmony wasn't going to be the next causality, not on his watch.

He called Fish and Monk; both of them were old timers who ran with Creed's father when he had been alive. Both of them had been aware of their plans two years ago, but Fish had asked them to wait for him to talk to her. Bringing a woman in as an old lady, especially a daughter of one of the old timers, was a big deal. Fish needed to tell the club he was okay with it. Creed had the upmost respect for the two older bikers because of their experience, but also because they are the scariest muther fuckers he had ever come across.

"You know I am gonna have your nuts in a vise for this," Harmony muttered and both men shook their heads and remained silent.

Monk walked into the office first and paused, raising an eyebrow at the sight of Harmony in handcuffs, but when Fish walked in, he laughed.

"How did you get my girl to stay in cuffs?" Fish said.

"Because I was waiting for a witness to kick their asses. Seriously, I didn't want to deal with the two drama kings here so I just waited," Harmony said with a shrug and stood and the cuffs dropped off her wrist. "Hey, Dad, Monk. I will let ya deal with them, I am going to say hi to Shady and Freedom, then I am outta here."

Monk clapped, Fish laughed harder, and Fork and Creed growled. "My baby girl has been able to get out of cuffs since she was knee high to a grasshopper," Fish roared. "You boys never listen or pay attention, do you?"

"No they don't, set them straight on this, Monk, and make sure they don't interfere again, or I am going to make sure to aim low with my gun," Harmony said and walked out the door. "Creed, Spoon, have a nice day and thanks for the tip," she said with a wink and she was gone.

"That is so uncool," Fork yelled. "You can't stab a guy with a spoon damn it."

Harmony slammed the door and both of them looked at Fish and Monk who were trying to keep a straight face. Creed rolled his eyes and then said.

"Fish, what is going on?"

The older man sighed and then ran a hand down his face. "We thought we had a handle on this, the two guys were feeling the pressure, we figured it was a matter of time before they gave us what we wanted. But we underestimated the leader of the Diablos; he isn't going to go away quietly. He wants this area for a pipeline and he is not going to give it up, put all of his eggs in one basket so he can't leave it. We are gonna have to figure out another way to get to them."

Monk nodded, "Savages asked for a meeting."

Creed felt Fork go stiff, *shit this was gonna be fun.* Fork and Tonto, the prez of the Savages, were half brothers, it was a long fucking boring story, but what it boiled down to was drama they didn't need right now. His best friend was gonna have to bury that shit for now.

"How are they involved, besides the obvious?" Creed said. When they had rescued Freedom from the Diablos, they discovered one of the Savages' women had been kidnapped as well.

"Got the same problem as we do, only they didn't catch any of the bastards, instead they got away. We are going to have to compare notes and make up a plan, their town is too close to ignore this, if we lose their town we are gonna be living with this shit forever, bleeding over into our business. It would be better if we cooperate with each other, and make them gone for good," Monk said and Creed looked at him closely.

The older biker reminded him of his father, long black hair that was turning silver now, was pulled back into a ponytail, his face weathered with age but still strong and tan. He respected the man, and Fish as well. He would listen to what they had to say, but his VP and best friend was going to have to put his shit aside or this wasn't going to work.

"Make the meet, we will be there," Creed said softly and then turned to Fish. "Harmony needs to be out of this, they have shown they will go after anyone who is a threat. She just put herself on the map and until we deal with this shit, she needs to lay low, she does that here."

"My daughter is not going to go for that and you know it. She made her choice two years ago when she stopped coming around. I tried to talk to her, but she said she was done with the club. Told you what her decision was, I won't betray her confidence. She is my daughter, I think I have some sorting out to do, didn't ask the right questions back then, just listened, and did what she said. Should have known better, club is in her blood," Fish smiled. "Even when she was pissed, not making sense and listening to reason, I should have paused. But I didn't, took her for her word and kept my promise. She is already knee deep in this shit, this became personal when they burned her office down. She is back, don't let her get away this time. And the last time I told my daughter anything, it did not go well for me, had to eat at

McDonalds for a week. So Monk and I will keep a lookout for her until we figure this out, just give me a few days."

Creed shook his head but Monk laughed. "Boy, I have been doing this for a long time, and I know how to handle Harmony. She will be fine."

Creed felt Fork move forward and lean in. "One week, then we are coming for her."

Monk frowned and Fish's eyes narrowed and looked at the president and vice president of the Ops Warriors Motorcycle Club closely. They apparently were shocked at what they saw because Fish began to shake his head.

"Not going there, man," Fish said quietly. "Last time was fucked up. Had my girl turned inside out, wouldn't talk to me, threatened to move if I didn't quit asking questions. I need to know before this goes further what the fuck she thinks happened. Because things *are not* adding up."

"I agree, we are not doing this again," Monk said then it was Creed and Fork's turn to look confused. Neither of them had any idea what the two older men were talking about, but they knew it had to do something with why Harmony hadn't been around for the last two years, and why she was so cold to them when she did show up.

"Not doing what?" Fork demanded. "We don't have a fucking clue what you are talking about."

Fish shook his head again. "Not my story to tell, but just know, not going there again because it almost broke her. Need to ask some questions, and until I do, Harmony doesn't want to be here, she is not here. Let her decide, and from what I can see, she already has. We can deal with the immediate and worry about the past later. Now, I am her father, Monk is her mentor, we have three other men who we can call to set up her protection and she has her men, the ones she employs. We will keep her safe."

"How many men does she employ?" Creed demanded, suddenly not liking that he and Fork hadn't kept up to date with what Harmony was doing the last few years. They had other things going on, and to be honest, neither of them thought she actually was doing anything other than running the office for Monk. Today, hearing that she was the boss, and not the secretary, didn't make them feel comfortable.

"Enough," Monk laughed and then said, "You wanna know about Hill Investigations, you gotta ask Harmony. But you gotta know though, she isn't going to like anyone questioning her business. She worked damn hard these last two years building her name in this business, she was young, and she knew it. So she made sure to surround herself with veteran people who she could trust. They made her look good, and she made them look good. They trust her, they will not fuck around with her safety, and she knows it. Hill Investigations is on the map as one of the best agencies in the country, we have calls from all over trying to get us to just consult, and Harmony takes every single one of their calls. She has a gift, one most men would love to have. She sees things most can't and she anticipates, makes it clear that she won't put up with people's shit, so she isn't going to put up with yours."

Creed and Fork had no idea how the hell they had missed this, they assumed—and wrongly, apparently—that Monk had been the one behind the show. Now they knew this was going to be more than trying to convince a headstrong female not to put herself in danger. They needed to convince a headstrong qualified female to allow them to help her. Not going to be good, but they were going to have to do it.

"Keep your eyes open, the Diablos aren't going to go away, and they are going to try to make a point however they have to. We need to make a point as well, the two little pissants you have mean nothing to them, but they are gonna use that. To make a stand against the law, for us, they are going to try to drive us out. Not happening," Creed said and Fork nodded.

*****

Shady was still asleep when Harmony came into the house. She had never been upstairs before, she had never been allowed. Well times were changing and she didn't care. Harmony took the stairs two at a time, looking at each floor as she went up. It was nothing special, she decided.

Over the years her mind had created a picture of what they looked like. A cross between a brothel and a biker bar had been what she dreamed up, but the clean cream-colored walls and nice décor wasn't what she expected.

When she arrived to the top floor she was further surprised, on the other floors doors were closed to each room for privacy. Apparently, up here, doors didn't matter. The whole place was open except for archways that led into bedrooms; this all surrounded a large family style area in the middle filled with sectionals and a television. The smaller kitchen was on the left as soon as you came up the stairs, and the large dining room table right in front of the stairs. A few of the guys were sitting and eating while Freedom was in the kitchen making what appeared to be pancakes. Poke and Easy were there, as was Raven. Creed and Fork were gone downstairs.

Everyone froze when she popped up the stairs.

"Harmony," Freedom cried and ran around the counter and hugged her. "Did we have a meeting?"

Hill Investigations was in charge of investigating Freedom's case. They had liked each other right off the bat, developing a friendship that wasn't just based on the case.

"Nah, looking for Shady." Harmony laughed. "Wanted to see my girl, been too long."

It had been, six weeks to be exact. Harmony felt bad when she didn't take Shady's calls two years ago. She had been devastated and heartbroken and wanted nothing to do with the club. So she had cut herself off, and when she tried to make amends with Shady a few months after she froze her out, it had been hard. Shady was not forgiving when it came to fucking up like she had. It was because of her childhood, and if Harmony had been in a better place, she would have known that.

Still, the struggle had been worth it, Shady was still her best friend. The last six weeks had been hard, they had only talked on the phone and not been able to hang out at all. Shady was the only person who knew what happened. Monk and her father only knew she decided to not be in the life two years ago. Shady had forgiven her and had also been pissed at the guys, but she had promised not to say anything, and when Shady promised something, it was solid.

"She is still asleep," Freedom said softly.

"Duh, I know." Harmony laughed. "This is Shady we are talking about."

"She isn't alone," Freedom whispered.

Harmony laughed louder and said, "Duh, this is Shady we are talking about."

Freedom bit her lip and Harmony rolled her eyes. Easy was the one who spoke up. "Harmony, you know you can't be up here."

"Fuck you, Easy," Harmony barked. She was happy for Freedom, she had found love with these two men, but it still didn't matter to Harmony, they were the same assholes they had always been.

Easy raised an eyebrow and looked at her with a steeled expression. "You know the rules," he said.

"Yeah, I know the rules, no one allowed up here without and invitation," Harmony said sarcastically. "SHAY!" she called.

"What?" Shady replied sleepily.

"Gimme a call when you wake up," Harmony yelled. "Fuckheads say I am not invited."

She heard her best friend swear and then she heard mumbling from the room right across for where she was standing. Giving Freedom a smile and the guys a glare, Harmony turned and ran down the stairs, she *so* didn't need this shit anymore. Fuckers, same as they always were, nothing was going to change, and she didn't have the time anymore to give a shit.

"Harmony," Shady called behind her. "Wait, girl."

Harmony reached the bottom floor and turned. Shady appeared wearing a t-shirt that barely hit the top of her thighs and her black long hair messed up and tangled, even at that, Shady was a knock out.

"Shay, just had a shitty night, even shittier morning and truthfully, I just wanted to talk to you for a second and see if you could come into town and see me," Harmony said sadly.

"You are invited to my room whenever, sorry I didn't tell them that, I will let them know," Shady said softly and Harmony nodded. *Goddamn old wounds*, she thought she had been over all this.

"Thanks," Harmony whispered.

"Now what the fuck is going on, you wouldn't step one toe on the compound unless something was fucked up," Shady said.

"Office was burned down, and I was just pissed off." Harmony shrugged.

Shady's eyes narrowed. "Diablos?"

Harmony nodded. "Yeah."

"Give me an hour, I will be at your place," Shady said and then turned, no other words were needed with them. Harmony knew Shady would be there when she said she would.

Chapter Three

"You have got to be fucking kidding me?" Shady yelled and paced the floor of her apartment. She had brought Freedom as well, because when Shady had gone back upstairs she had lit into the men that were there.

Freedom had been just as pissed and then when her men, along with the others that were there, said Harmony wasn't allowed on their floor no matter if Shady invited her or not, it had gotten bad. Creed and Fork had come into a screaming match and Shady and Freedom went off the deep end when the two leaders backed the men.

Now all three women were in Harmony's apartment, having called the others who were on their way. They were picking up provisions.

Harmony had just told them what had happened that last night, and then both girls had exploded. Shady because she knew the situation and Freedom because she had been clued in when she got there, and was still freaking pissed at her men.

"Those assholes," Freedom announced and stood. "No fucking sex for them, they can sleep on the damn couch."

"Free," Harmony said softly. "They can't know I heard that."

"Fuck that, those assholes, they tell everyone the club is a family and shit, and then they say stuff like that about one of their own. What is wrong with them? Would it have been so hard to quietly take you aside and talk to you, not stand at a party full of people and talk about you like that," Freedom yelled.

Harmony shrugged. "Dad did talk to me, I just thought he was worried though, I didn't know Creed had asked him. I felt like a dumbass."

"Exactly," Shady said firmly. "They didn't come to you, they let your dad tell you, and I would bet they didn't tell him that it was because you were crushing on Creed and Fork."

"Oh my God, this is embarrassing. I mean, I heard what they said, I got over it, but still, even after being gone and shit, I am still not good enough for them, or even for you," Harmony said.

That is why she had been upset and not answered Shady's calls two years ago. When she had heard what they said, yes she knew they were talking about her crush, but she had also convinced herself that none of them thought of her as someone who was trustworthy. They should have stood up for her, or at the least given her a heads up. It hurt to know they all felt the same, Raven and Rock had been at her graduation for God's sake, it was like a punch in the gut knowing they were just there because they had to be.

"You know, fuck this," Shady said and looked at the other two women. "I get the Warriors are a club. I get that we belong to the club, but they let us make our own decisions, like with Trick. *We* had to deal with that shit because they don't hurt women. I respect that, but some women need to be hurt. But they can't have it both ways."

"Club rules, always been like that." Harmony shrugged. "In fact, before you came in, Shay, they didn't deal with women like at all. They were just a hole to fill. I saw it every single day."

"That is whacked," Shady said. "Leather and Lace has been around for a long time, like twenty years. Female biking clubs are not unheard of. I mean, why can't we have Warrior Bitches, we could be a sub-chapter of the Ops Warriors."

The women were silent, it was like a light bulb went off in the room. They would have the protection of the club, but they would also have the ability to set the rules for the women in the club. Because honestly, the skanks that kept showing up and causing problems were pissing them all right the fuck off. The girls danced at the club and brought in business; they were the ones putting themselves on the line.

Harmony's doorbell rang and Free jumped up and answered the door. Rain, Treat, Nike, and Bob walked into the room. These women were the ones who danced, who stepped forward in the club and claimed a place for themselves, they weren't the club whores, the hang arounds, they were part of the Warriors, they didn't have a vote in club business, and they didn't care, but they did handle a lot of shit for the club. Hell, Shady ran the gun storage/shipping business. She reported to Creed but she was in charge. The guys needed to back the fuck off some of this shit. They knew their place, they always would, the Ops Warriors weren't an equal opportunity club. They were too thick headed to be that progressive. But they couldn't argue with the stuff they already did, including dishing out punishment to women who betrayed the club.

"What up, chickies?" Rain asked, carrying a twelve pack of Mike's Hard Lemonade.

"Yeah, what was the 911?" Bob asked.

"We got an issue," Shady said and Harmony looked around the room, as the women's faces got hard as they heard what had happened. Shady had even told them what happened in the past, and it was Bob who surprised her. The small woman with curves and a mean temper had been pissed off about that.

"Seriously?" she yelled. "I even knew that Harmony was the one behind the investigations, damn, all they had to do was pay attention. Who did they think found half of the shit they needed online?"

"What do you mean?" Shady said and Harmony closed her eyes. She knew what was coming, Bob was the oldest of the women; she had been there a long time.

"Shay, really? These boys would go into Church and talk about all the stuff. Then they would all come out with shit that needed to be done, and all of them—every single one of the old timers—would go right to Harmony. Since she was a kid, she has been able to find shit out on the net, hell, who do you think mapped out our delivery routes, did it when she was fifteen, took the cops routes and ran some program to see which roads were the safest. Then when Creed and the others took over she would just listen, overhear stuff, and suddenly one of the Prospects would get information. I mean seriously, all they had to do was ask, but no, the

Prospects took the credit, damn, Harmony got more than one of those boys their patches," Bob snorted.

All of the girls turned and looked at Harmony. "What?" she asked loudly.

"Why didn't you ever say anything?" Shady asked.

Harmony shrugged and looked around. "What? I am good at finding stuff, figured the club would need the information. I don't need any pats on the back."

"But your father and Monk, they had to know, why didn't they say anything?" Shady asked.

"They didn't figure it out for a while, and when they did, I begged them not to tell. Both of them figured one of the guys would fess up, none of them did, and so I just kept quiet." Harmony laughed.

"Settles it," Shay announced. "Operation Bitches is in effect. We need to come up with a bunch of shit to present to the club at one of the first available meetings. I am not fucking around with this shit, they do not tell me anymore who can come into my bedroom. In fact, I say we have our own freaking floor, they can expand off the back, not like we don't have the money, shit, I have the money to do it."

"Harmony needs a name," Freedom said.

"You don't have one." Harmony laughed.

"Yeah, but they all call me Free, same thing," Freedom said.

"Then call me Harm." Harmony shrugged.

"Um no," Shady said and looked around the room. "We can come up with something better, because when you have a nickname, it means you are in. Trust me, you are not a Prospect for the Warrior Bitches, you are all in, you paid your dues."

Everyone nodded and Harmony laughed, it was the first time in all of her life with the Warriors that she actually felt like she belonged to something, she was no longer Fish's daughter, she was a Bitch.

*****

"Monk called," Fork said as he walked into the offices. Creed was the only one in there for the moment, and he was glad, they needed to talk about shit.

"Yeah?" Creed said and looked at Fork closely.

"Tonto agreed to the meet, wants it to happen sooner rather than later, so this weekend," Fork said.

"You cool with that?" Creed said.

Fork laughed. "Wasted a lot of time with all that shit a long time ago, not wasting anymore. He wants to be pissed he can, I didn't make that call, and as far as I can see, he may not think he got the better end of the deal, but shit. Live with my fucking asshole father and crazy bitch mother for a few years and he'd see how lucky he was."

Creed knew all about Fork's childhood, they'd been best friend since grade school. Creed had seen the bruises and witnessed the crazy. All it had proven to Creed was even the wealthy had problems behind closed doors. When Limbo had offered Fork a place to stay on more than one occasion, it had become clear to Creed that Fork's parents were fucked. Fork tried to make contact with Tonto when he was eighteen, but the older man refused to speak to him, Fork had just blown it off. Tonto's hatred for he and Fork's mother bled over into the club, it pissed Creed off. He refused to do any business with the Savages because of it. It made the tension between the two clubs run high, and when other shit was going on, like the Diablos, it made the situation volatile. They had no clue if the Savages were even going to want to play ball, it was logical, but the shit between Fork and Tonto was anything but logical.

"Yeah," Creed said and then said, "Harmony."

"Shit, man, did you see her?" Fork said and ran his hand through his hair. "Fish would gut me if he knew what I was thinking 'bout his little girl."

"Yeah, me too," Creed said.

"Can't fucking believe this, her coming in here throwing fucking attitude, it was fucked. She is the one who froze us out," Fork said.

Creed nodded. "Yeah, her ass is fucking more amazing than it was before."

"What do you think about what they said about Hill?" Fork asked. He knew his friend had to be shocked, fuck, all of the guys had been when they sat and talked about it on the floor earlier.

Hearing that Harmony was a little badass didn't make any of them feel any better. They all wanted to do right by her, shit, he could still remember a few years ago when they found out she was opening a PI office. It had shocked them, but then they also had assumed that Fish was the one who set her up, he hadn't. Didn't mean they didn't support her, hell, before she refused to take their calls, Creed and Fork were prepared to let her run this business through the club, get to know her, and make their intentions known. Then she was fucking gone, just gone, and they had been pissed.

During college, Harmony had done an internship for some big agency. She had solved a major case and gotten a reward, used the money to start up her business. They had been proud of her, and were going to tell the guys their intentions. But one of the girls who was a dancer had to be taken care of before they could do that. The woman had been seriously wacked, Lola had been obsessed with Creed and Fork, thought she was their woman. Shit, they found out she was selling drugs in their club, in their fucking name, telling people it was Warriors drugs. It was all wacked, they had a party to set Lola up, and then sent her away. Creed and Fork were ready to make Harmony theirs and she disappeared. Not from the town, from them.

"We are missing something, one minute we were going to have a meeting, had the guys from the other chapters so we could do the vote and be done with it. Then Fish came and said Harmony refused to come to the compound, it was fucked up. No one would talk to us, and then Fish cancelled the vote. You know as well as I do, it is club rules, we can't do anything unless Fish agrees, he said no, we had to back off. Now? Fuck this, something is going on and I want to know what. I will respect Fish and Monk, but they need to give us an answer. If they don't, I am calling Shady in, she can talk to Harmony for us."

Chapter Four

Dominic Reyes looked at the book in front of him. This wasn't going fast enough, they had obligations to the cartel in Mexico, and they were about ready to fucking lose a whole lot of money if they couldn't open the pipeline for delivery.

The Warriors and the Savages were a pain in his ass. All they had to do was look the other way, fucking bastards. The Diablos had connections. Those connections wanted a place to bring women, drugs, and guns without hassle. Took them a long time to find this little highway, the connection to all the major highways in the U.S. The perfect road, because no one patrolled it, and his sister had led him right to it. It ran right along the border of two states, right to the center of the country, the perfect place they would be able to distribute easily, and the cartel was not accepting no. Dom found it by accident, looking for his long lost bitch of a sister who had ruined his life.

The two idiots who were in custody didn't matter to him. The nosy PI who was asking questions that made him nervous. He didn't need his cover to be blown right now; no one even knew he was in town. His woman, Lola, had been smart, she had covered their tracks years ago. It made it easier to come and go from town when they thought you were an upstanding citizen; of course, Lola was covering the Savages, she couldn't show her face here again after those assholes threw her out of town. It didn't matter; they were still going to get what they wanted.

They were on a timeframe; a large shipment was coming to replace the goods they lost. If the PI kept asking questions, they were going to have to take care of business with her, as well as take on the Warriors.

He hadn't told the cartel about the mines, Lola and he had a plan; it was going to take him out of the business and set them for life. But they had to play the games for right now, and losing money and shipments wasn't smart.

"We need to make sure the shipment gets into town without anyone noticing. No more fuckups, if you can't handle one little female and some lowlife bikers, then you are in the wrong business," Dom yelled at one of the men who were standing in front of him. They nodded and left.

Dom stood and pulled the gun from where it was resting on the shelf, he had this gun since he was a child; his father showed him how to shoot this gun. Hell, he had killed his father with the gun, and then he had done exactly what his mother wanted. Find his sister and make her pay. Little bitch thought she was done with him, with the family, fuck that. She owed him, and she was going to pay.

*****

"Harmony," her father called. Shit, she had a hangover. Yesterday she and the girls had completely gotten blitzed. It had been fun. Felt like old times with the girls being there for her.

She lifted her head and looked, Shady and Freedom were in bed with her, they had stayed over, fuck they had all stayed over. The other girls were in the spare room.

With a groan she rolled over. The guys had been pissed when Freedom and the others had called and said they were staying in town. Not telling them why, but Easy and Poke had been suspicious; when they called Free to check in, she had been wasted and called them Neanderthals. It had been funny at the time, but they had been confused, then came to town to get Free. She had done some fancy footwork to get them to go home.

"Harmony," her dad called again.

"Dad, hang on," Harmony called and Shady moaned and rolled over.

"What the fuck?" Shady whispered.

"Dad, I will get rid of him," Harmony said and rolled from the bed. She didn't look in the mirror at all, it wasn't going to be pretty, and she was *not* in the mood.

As she stumbled out the door of her room her father took a step back and froze, she looked at his face out of one eye and frowned. "Dad, come on, it's too early for a visit. Come back later and we can talk about what we need to do."

He burst out laughing and she frowned and glared at him. "What?"

"Honey, I hate to ask, but why do you have a tattoo on your forehead?" her father said.

Harmony slapped a hand to her forehead and moaned, shit, what had they done last night. She ran for a mirror and stared at herself in horror. As she leaned closer she breathed a sigh of relief, she remembered. It was marker, not real ink—thank God. They were designing the new tat for the Warrior Bitches and Rain had pulled out a marker, said they needed to see it on skin to make sure they liked it. Fuck, how had it gotten on her forehead. Whatever, she needed a shower.

"Dad, I gotta get cleaned up and shit, give me a few hours and I will come into your office. I will call Monk and have him meet us, we have a lot of shit to go over." Harmony yawned.

"Honey, we need to talk about something first," her dad said seriously. Shit, she wasn't in the mood for one of his heart to hearts.

"Not now, Dad," Harmony said. "I promise, let me get cleaned up, drink a huge amount of coffee, and come to the office, we can go to dinner later and talk." She felt his hesitation and looked at him. "What?"

"Just tell me," her father said softly. "Two years ago, when you came home crying. I asked you if someone had hurt you. You said no, but that you were done with the club, it wasn't the life you wanted. Said you wanted more."

Harmony frowned, she had been upset that night, knowing how the guys felt it had crushed her, but she didn't want her dad to go after them so she told him what he needed to hear. She had grown up, and realized that club life wasn't for her.

"Yeah, Dad," Harmony said softly. She wasn't going to tell him the truth now; it would be a waste of time.

"Honey, what happened to make you change your mind. You went to the party. I figured it got out of hand, scared you," her father said and Harmony laughed and rolled her eyes.

"Dad, really, come on, scared me," she said like it was a joke.

"But you were crying," her dad said and looked at her confused.

She had a hangover, the guys pissed her off, and she had no more patience for this stuff. "Yeah, I was crying, the assholes said I was a pain in the ass and they didn't want me hanging around."

"They said that to you directly?" her dad said with a smile, which irritated her a bit more.

"Dad, did you hear what I said. They wanted me gone, away, no more hanging around. I was a pest, so it hurt. No, I didn't get that from them, they were too chicken shit to say it to me, I heard them all talking. Man, you are my dad, I didn't tell you because I thought you would be pissed, but damn this is not even cool you laughing at me," she yelled.

"Oh, honey," her father said and kissed her forehead. "Get dressed and come to the office. We need to talk."

"Whatever," Harmony said, "I will be there in a few," pissed her father was acting like that.

*****

"Yeah, you need to come to the house in a half an hour," Fish said as he walked out of his daughter apartment building.

"What's up, Fish?" Fork asked and then he heard Creed in the background asking the same thing.

"Harmony," was all he said and laughed.

*****

"This is so gonna piss me off," Harmony snapped when she went back into her room. Free and Shay rolled over with a groan.

"Dying," Free said huskily.

"Yeah, wishing for death more like it," Shay mumbled and then screeched when Harmony slammed a pillow down on her head.

"Bitch, this is serious. My father wants a meeting, and I need to get the shit back together with the investigation.

Plus we need to figure out what the fuck is going on with the club," Harmony snipped.

"Butterfly," Free said.

"Huh?" Harmony replied, looking down at her friend thinking she was still drunk.

"Your club name, Butterfly." Free laughed and rolled over and got off the bed. They had passed out last night in their clothes.

No one should look that good rolling out of bed with wrinkled clothes and messed up hair but this chick, fuck.

"Do I look like a fucking Butterfly?" Harmony snapped.

"Yeah, not so much right now." Shady laughed from the bed. "You look like Killer Clowns."

"Ugh," Harmony said, remembering she had the ink on her forehead. "Showering, and then out in ten. You all need to figure out how we are dealing with shit today."

"Yeah, Poke and Easy are going to be here soon, I can tell you that." Free mumbled, "Assholes."

"Don't be too hard on them, they were just following Creed and Fork's attitude about me," Harmony warned.

"Still assholes," Shady muttered, stood, and hugged Harmony. "We are going back to the club, come out when you are done, we will talk some more, but we are laying down the law when we get there. That is my home too."

Harmony smiled at her best friend and nodded. "Don't get too pissy because of me, I am a big girl, I can handle it."

She could too; it was just nice to finally feel like someone had her back. For the last two years it had been the guys she worked with, and truthfully, none of them knew how much chocolate was required when you were PMSing, some of them just brought one candy bar, it sucked.

Harmony went to the bathroom and showered, refusing to look in the mirror yet again until she had scrubbed her face with a washcloth. But it gave her time to think. The Diablos were giving her a warning; she just didn't understand what it meant. Sure, they had two of their guys but they weren't talking, so they basically had no information whatsoever. Her questioning the members of the gang was normal. With these cases, if the people in custody wanted to take the fall for their gang they did. No other information was shared. It was always the same, and she knew this, they had to as well. Which is why it didn't make sense, all they had to do was lay low for a few weeks and shit would blow over. Sneaky little bastards should know enough about the drug trade to know this.

By burning her office they were trying to send a message, and one that was really not needed. Why put yourself on the map by actually making a statement like that. Hell, for all they knew the two idiots they had in custody could be the leaders of the gang, highly unlikely because they were idiots, but still.

She was missing something about this case, and it was bothering her. Harmony was all about the puzzles, it was how her mind worked. That was what made her a good investigator; she never gave up until the last question was answered. This was something her father had taught her.

She got out of the shower, wrapped herself in a robe, then set to work on her hair and make-up. She looked like hell, and she would get a lot of shit if she didn't hide the bags under her eyes.

By the time she was ready, she had mentally gone over the last few weeks and completely done an inventory of what information they had. Still, none of it fit together, they were going to need to get some more information out of the two Diablos they had. Shitheads were making it hard for them though, refusing to talk to them when they went to the jail. It was pissing her off.

As she walked into her living room, she took in the scene. All of the girls were laying on her couches and chairs moaning about feeling like shit. She would have laughed, but she figured it would hurt their heads. She was wearing her normal Levi jeans, black tank, and black work boots with a steel toe. Her long hair pulled back into a high ponytail that swung when she walked. All in all, she looked a shit ton better than what her friends did.

"Bitch," Bob said when she caught sight of her. "Why are you looking all perky and we feel like ass?"

"'Cause I am amazing," Harmony said and walked toward the door. "Coffee is in the kitchen, food in the fridge, make yourselves at home. If you leave lock the door, I have a key."

"Flush," Shady called out and Harmony paused and turned around.

"Excuse me?" she said confused.

"Your club name, Flush, you know, like I am gonna flush your head in the toilet for looking so good." Shady laughed.

"How about, Swirly." Treat laughed and Harmony rolled her eyes and walked out of the apartment.

Club names were important, they defined who you were, and all had a story to tell. She only hoped she wasn't going to end up with a fucked up name when all was said and done.

Chapter Five

Creed and Fork rolled into Fish's home office. They hoped they finally were going to get same answers about Harmony, because after last night, hearing the women were all over at Harmony's and they were in an uproar, things weren't looking good on that front.

Fish was smiling when they walked in and he motioned for them to sit down. A half an hour later, the two leaders were sitting in the room waiting for their woman to come. They had been shocked and pissed when they heard what Harmony had said. After promising to tell Harmony that her father had a meeting, he left and they were there waiting.

"Gonna paddled her ass," Fork growled. "How the fuck were we supposed to know she was standing there. She should have said something."

"She didn't trust us," Creed snapped.

"Paddling hard so she remembers," Fork said and his friend nodded.

They heard the click of the front door and both sucked in a breath and waited.

"Dad," Harmony called. "Why are you here, thought we were meeting at the... Shit."

The guys knew she had seen them and before she could turn and leave, they were on the move. Creed grabbed her arms and pulled her into the room while Fork slammed the office door and locked it.

"What?" she started to say and Creed held up his hand.

"Two years," Creed said quietly. Harmony had no idea what they were talking about and so she kept her mouth shut and waited, they were going to have to give her a bit more information than that.

"Two years, babe," Fork repeated and she rolled her eyes, so they were speaking in code, she got it.

"Two years," Harmony mimicked. "Yeah, I got that, now move on, I have things to do and you obviously have something to talk to me about."

"Wasted two years waiting for you to pull your head out of your ass and tell us what the fuck was going on. But did you, *no*. Fish had to tell us that you overheard something and that you didn't get right, got pissed and never asked a question. Instead, you freeze us out, and we are clueless," Creed roared. "Two fucking years, babe, we could have been fucking like bunnies instead of Fork and me jacking off to the thought of your sweet little pussy. Wishing that chicks we were fucking were you, and waiting."

Harmony's eyes narrowed. "Seriously, you did not just say you were fucking other women and thinking about me, and I am supposed to what, take that as a compliment?"

"No, you should have clued into the fact I am pissed off you made assumptions about something that *was not* the facts and froze us out. You should be asking what the fuck you heard us talking about," Fork yelled.

"Uh, excuse me here," Harmony snapped and looked at the two men like they were crazy. "Can you actually pause for a second and explain yourselves because right now, you don't make any sense."

"Clue into this, babe, two years ago, you overheard a conversation that had nothing to do with you and everything to do with a bitch we were outing from the club, and for some reason you took that in and twisted it. Instead of asking one fucking question, you made an assumption about it," Creed said and Harmony's eyes went wide.

"Not about me?" she whispered.

"No, babe, remember, Lola." Fork smiled.

"Yeah," she whispered.

"She was selling drugs in the club, telling people she had permission, telling them it was for the club. Then she wanted us, kept appearing in our rooms and shit. We needed to get her out of there before we made the announcement that we were claiming our own chick," Creed growled.

"Your own chick," Harmony whispered.

"Yeah, babe, we had a plan," Fork said.

"Well clue the fuck in. I don't give a shit about your plan, Spoon," Harmony snapped as she realized they were expecting her to be happy about this discussion.

"You should, since the plan included you!" Creed yelled.

"You can't kill someone with a fucking spoon damn it!" Fork yelled at the same time and she jumped and tried to sort what they were saying.

"What plan would include me?" Harmony demanded.

"We are the leaders of a MC club, babe, we have rules, and one of the rules is that the kid of an old timer is off limits unless he gives permission. To do that, he has to talk to the club and tell them he approves. Fish was gonna do that the day after the party you busted and overheard shit you were not supposed to overhear. After Fish made his announcement then we tell everyone we are taking a shot at you," Creed said calmly.

Harmony rolled this around in her head and then nodded. "Okay, cool. That all?"

"That all?" Fork asked confused. They had just told her that she fucked up, and all she could say was "that all?"

"Yeah, Spoon, that all. I have shit to do today and then I have a meeting with a new client. That all?"

"What the fuck, babe!" Creed yelled.

"Stop calling me Spoon!" Fork yelled.

"Listen, I appreciate you clearing that whole thing up for me, but I don't know what you want from me now, you obviously moved on, fucking other women and all. I have moved on, it is over, you weren't talking about me, cool." Harmony shrugged their hands off her and walked to the door calmly.

"That all you have to say? Are you fucking with me right now?" Creed said quietly.

"Yeah, that is all I have to say. Because one, let me make this clear to you. I have a brain. You going to the club and my father and never giving me the heads up about wanting a shot with me is fucking archaic!" she yelled.

"Babe, we knew you wanted a shot with us." Fork laughed.

Harmony opened her mouth and then closed it, pissed they had known she was interested in them and never once let on they returned her attraction. *What fucking assholes.*

"I am done," Harmony yelled.

"Done?" Creed said.

"Yeah, done. I was interested, now I am not. So thanks for clearing that up for me but I am done. This is bullshit," Harmony said. "Open the fucking door."

Fork smiled and walked to where she was standing and grabbed her hand, before she knew it he was kissing her, and not a peck on the cheek, it was a hot, wet, full action, tongue kiss, intended to prove to her how much she still wanted them. *Fuck, it did too.* When Fork released her, Creed moved in and kissed her the same, hard, fast, and sizzling. *Shit, she couldn't think.* Then he let her go and she stumbled. Fork grinned again, opened the door, and pushed her into the hallway.

"Babe, you had better be at the compound at seven tonight. Announcement will be made, and if you are not there and we have to come looking for you, it is gonna be bad," Fork warned.

Harmony finally found her voice and she glared at the two men who were grinning at her.

"Thanks for the social update, Spoon, but I have plans tonight," Harmony snapped and then walked out the door. Damned if she didn't have to make a detour to change her underwear, they made her so hot.

"You think she will be there?" Fork grinned.

Creed laughed and turned to his friend. "No, that is what's gonna make this fun. Let's go, need to get to the meeting with the Savages."

*****

Fork stared at his half-brother. Creed had asked for a few minutes alone with just the four men who were in the room. Tonto, his VP, Sandman, Creed, and him. It was tense, and also a long time coming.

"We gonna be able to bury this?" Fork asked.

They hadn't gotten too far in depth with this situation, it was going to take a while, but what it boiled down to was that both their fathers were pricks, and neither of them had any control over what happened when they were young. It happened, it was over, and they needed to move on. They were blood.

"Yeah," Tonto said with a sigh. "Leave the past buried."

"Good," Creed said. "We need to get the others in here. A lot of shit to talk about, man."

Sandman grinned. "We gonna have more to bury than the past. Fuckers are going to go down."

Creed nodded and then opened the door and motioned for the rest of the guys to come in. There was only eight of them total, four from each side; it was what was agreed upon.

"Let's get down to business," Creed said and nodded to Poke and Easy, the other two who were at the meeting.

"Our woman got caught up in the mess, we want payback," Easy said smoothly. "They have been running shit through our town and causing some serious issues with our distribution. What has been going on with you?"

"Selling laced drugs to high school students," Sandman said and the guys nodded. "Gotta get them outta of the fucking town, kids going down faster than we can get it off the street. Sucks."

They all had a code they lived by, it was good to know that both clubs felt the same way about drugs, they didn't run them, anything else was on the table, but with the mine, the Warriors had not had to worry about money, they were distributing needed hardware to people who needed it. End of story. They were also well aware of the Savages' underground fighting clubs. They were impressive.

The Warriors needed to make sure their guns were getting to the places they were needed. It was a little known fact the guns they supplied helped keep the order on the streets. Also, they were given to people who needed protection, mostly abused women. But the majority of their money was made in the mines, and the running of the mines was consuming. Also, dealing with the other club properties took time, they needed to get the situation under control with the Diablos. The strip club had been taking up a lot of

Prospects' guard time. The bar was also having to be watched, and Slinging Ink was only open by appointment only right now. The jobs were divided but at the meeting following this one, they were going to be sorted and assigned for the foreseeable future, Creed was sick of reacting to the fucking Diablos, now it was their turn to push the fuck back and give them a statement. They didn't want to fuck with the Warriors and the Savages, they needed to move on.

"How do you want to play this?" Tonto asked.

"Get the clubs together, make sure everyone is on the same page, we don't need anymore of this shit between us," Creed said and Fork nodded and stared at Tonto who agreed. "Then we go on the offensive, this shit is gonna stop."

By the end of the meeting, they had their plan, party this weekend at the Warriors club. Then the Savages had reciprocated with inviting them to a cookout at their club. With the shit about to get real, they all needed to be prepared and show a united front.

First course of action, they needed the two little fucks in jail to start talking. Tonto agreed and after this weekend, they would have some answers. The party was gonna provide alibis.

Chapter Six

It was late; the sun was getting ready to set when she was finally done with her day. The meeting with the two Diablos was a bust again. Harmony had sat in a small room, with two smelly men who apparently didn't think showering was a good idea in jail. She could still smell the grossness as she walked out of the jail. After her informative meeting this morning with her men at their new offices, AKA the Starbucks on the corner across from the old offices. She had been frustrated.

No one knew a damn thing about who burned their offices down. The cameras had all been disabled, and no leads were coming in. They knew it was the Diablos; however, they couldn't prove it. The investigation for Free was stalled and basically they were chasing their tails, it pissed her off. She knew there was something she was missing, but she wasn't seeing it, no matter how many times her and her guys brainstormed.

Right now, most of her men were out on a job, the only ones left at the home base were Monk, Jimmy, and Simon. They were all looking for clues on the street for what was going on. So far, nothing. Feeling frustrated and pissed off, Harmony was on her way home, she was more than ready for this day to be over with. It sucked having a hangover when you had shit to do, because it made everything more difficult. She needed a shower, a tall glass of water, and a good night's sleep.

As she approached her apartment building, Harmony should have known she was off. And by off she meant that her normal senses that warned her of danger were hung over and asleep, because she completely missed the two pissed off bikers that were waiting for her.

Harmony pulled on the door to the lobby, suddenly she was in the air with an arm wrapped around her waist pulling her toward the road and she freaked and screamed.

"What the fuck?" she said as she started to struggle to see who had their hands on her.

"Told you to be at the club at seven," Creed barked out.

Harmony relaxed when she heard his voice and hung her head. Damn it, she was so not going to get into this right now.

"Creed," she said tiredly.

"No," Fork said in a hard tone. "We tell you to be somewhere, your ass is there."

Harmony narrowed her eyes. "You did not just say that to me."

Creed stopped and released her from around the waist and turned her so she was facing the two very pissed off men. "Yeah, Harmony, I did," Fork snarled. "We do not chase our woman around fucking town when she is supposed to be somewhere with us."

"Your woman?" she yelled. "I am not your woman."

"Once again, babe, you need to clue in. Talked to you this morning and told you that we were doing this. Already have permission, we stated our intentions, everyone knows you are claimed and under our protection. No more fucking around, we wasted two years, two fucking years because you didn't ask us what was going on," Creed leaned in and said to her.

Shit, she thought as she shivered, *that was fucking hot*. She was not experienced but damn, she felt herself get a little wet from his tone, but fuck him. She needed to change her underwear again, fuck. Then he leaned down and kissed her, this wasn't the hard claiming they had done earlier today, this was a soul-searching knock-you-off-your-feet kiss that she could feel all the way to her toes. He slid his tongue across the seam of her lips, and then plunged in, making her bend backwards from the pressure of his lips. He coaxed, branded, and seared her. When he eased his mouth off hers, Fork took over. Not giving her a chance to breathe, he eased his mouth over hers and then teased her lips, biting and tasting her until she moaned into his mouth.

Shit, she thought when they raised her up, she needed to get control of this situation, or they were going to think they had won.

"Uh," Harmony said quietly at first, gaining more momentum and thoughts, they couldn't just kiss the shit out of her every single time they wanted. "So not working for me, guys. One, I don't follow orders well. Two, I don't follow orders well. And three, I DON'T FUCKING FOLLOW ORDERS VERY WELL!"

"You *will* learn," Fork said and Harmony felt her blood pressure rising. Then before she knew it, Fork turned her and put her on the back of Creed's motorcycle. He gave her a quick kiss and then turned to grab something, Creed turned, grinned, and kissed her as well.

Shit, they couldn't keep kissing her like this.

She moved as if to get off, Creed grabbed her leg, and Fork leaned over and whispered in her ear, "Babe, holding on by a fucking string, so don't piss me off anymore than I am right now. You lift that ass off Creed's ride and you will not be able to sit down for a fucking week."

Harmony crossed her arms across her chest and refused to hold on to Creed. Fork shoved a helmet on her head, while Creed just sat and waited for Fork to get on his bike. The VP turned and glared at Harmony and waited. Finally, she let out a puff of breath and grabbed the side of his shirt. Creed reached up and pulled her arms around him until she was wrapped around him and she sighed again. *Assholes*, she thought.

They drove through town and Harmony had a moment to actually think, it wasn't a long time, because Creed and Fork both were going like a bat out of hell to get to the compound. When they pulled up to the main house, people were waiting. Her father was right in the front, grinning. She knew what this was, her father had told her about it when she was young because she had been present when one of the members brought their new old lady home. This was the welcoming of a new member.

Fucking A, so not happening.

She got off the bike slowly, then Creed pulled off her helmet and before she knew it she was standing with both men at her side, and they grabbed her hands and moved her to the crowd. She searched it and found Shady who was frowning, and the other girls who had their arms crossed over their chests and were frowning as well.

"Harmony," her father said. "We talked and the club has decided that you need to remain on the compound until we figure out why you are being targeted."

She was silent; there was no fucking way this was happening. They did not run her life, they would never run her life, and she would never *allow* them to run her life.

They mistakenly took her silence as acceptance, because he continued speaking. "I know this is hard, honey, but the club agrees with me. This is going to get really bloody, they have already proven what they will do, and we just need to be safe. The guys from Hill will be allowed on the compound, they are gonna set you up an office for now because yours is trashed, so this will work out, you will see."

Harmony just stared forward showing no reaction, but inside she was fuming. Monk stepped up and her gaze swung to him. "I already forwarded all the calls to the landline here, we can have new computers set up tomorrow, be back in business tomorrow night. It is the only way, Harmony, I agreed with your dad, especially since you don't know the other things that are going on, you need to trust me on this."

Other things she didn't know, that translated into club business, which translated into shit she didn't need to worry about. They would never let her in on club business. She saw Shady and the girls shoving their way to the front of the pack. She needed them before she completely blew and began screaming at these men. It wouldn't look good for her father or for her. Women didn't disrespect the members like that, she knew that, was taught that since she was young.

"Smurf," Bob called out and Harmony closed her eyes, damn it.

"Who is Smurf?" Monk asked loudly, looking around.

"Never mind," Bob muttered, obviously she was trying to break the ice. They could see how tense she was.

Shady stepped forward, "Maybe you all need a clue, why don't we go inside and talk about this, impromptu meeting of the whole Warriors."

Creed and Fork looked over her head, Harmony felt the tug on her hand, and she followed. Not wanting to open her mouth or she was going to fucking scream.

They led her into the main room, all of the members who were present followed, and they sat down and waited. She knew this was not church, this was informal, because if it were church they would be in the meeting room, so to this, she was thinking the men in this club didn't take them seriously.

Shady looked at the people in the room, and from the tightness of her lips, she knew what Harmony was thinking too.

"Shady," Creed said as he and Fork led her to the bar and stood in front of the room.

"The Bitches talked. We have decided we are making a women's chapter of the Warriors MC. We deserve it, we are in accordance to your rules, and we have always followed your lead. However, we also clean up the messes the other women in the club make because you all don't want to cross that line. We don't have a problem with it, and will never have a problem with it, however, we think we also could benefit the club with some of the stuff we already do, but we can also take over. Bob and Rain both have management training. I already run the Shop. We are a charter to the Warriors, we have our own church, we deal with the families, and the other shit," Shady said.

"What about our rules?" Creed said reasonably. "That will not change, we have rules that have been around here for a long time. Not that we don't respect what you have to say, but we have always done it this way."

"We will follow your rules, we are just asking to set rules of our own," Shady countered.

The room was silent and then Creed said, "Next meeting, we will discuss it, let you know what we think.

Before then, have something written down we can look at. But I will tell you right now, if it involves you not following our rules, it will not fly. Right now, the women are on lockdown until we figure out what's going on. If you leave here, you have an escort, and then it will be two men. Phones and GPS on all the time. We are having a party next week with the Savages, they are coming here, and we need to do this big. And when I say big, I mean I need all hands on deck, we will make them feel welcome. Call the whores and get them in line. We are being watched and want to send the message the clubs are united this matter."

Shady frowned but nodded and Creed continued, "After the meeting, we are going to have a plan on how we are going to take out the Diablos. This shit needs to end. I am sick of this. Before the party we are gonna try to get some answers."

"How are we going to do that?" Bob said innocently. Harmony knew where this was going and she was going to watch this play out without saying a word right now.

"The men have their assignments," Creed said as if that answered everything.

"Yeah, I know, but I need to know for Harmony who has what, considering besides the last two years, she has been the one to gather the Intel in the club. All of the assignments the Prez and VP would give the guys they asked Harmony for help. She would do her thing on the Internet and give them what they needed," Bob said stoically. "I thought I would help a sister out, you know, since this is kinda time sensitive. So after this is all done, form a line and we can organize for Harmony."

Creed and Fork jerked a little and you could have heard a pin drop in the room. Fish cleared his throat and said, "Well yeah, I used her for a few things in the past, but nothing that was off limits."

Monk laughed. "Hell used, bribed her with candy bars when she was young, she knows how to work a computer."

"Hacked into the county mainframe and got the reports on the mine for me," Raven shrugged. "Gave her a bottle of Jack."

Fish frowned. "Wait, how old was she?"

"Seventeen, wanted to have party she said." Raven laughed.

"Yeah, helped me out with finding a way around the border laws when we needed weapons," someone else said. And on and on it went until the room fell silent.

Harmony looked at the men in the room, the tension was thick, something was going on here, and she wasn't sure exactly what it was, but she also didn't care right now. She was still pissed and she needed to have a moment with the girls to talk to them. So she stood, walked to her friend, and held out her hand. All of the men misconstrued what was happening, and let them.

Because when Shady took her hand, they walked to Free and got her, then Bob, Rain, Treat, and Nike, then they filed out of the room. Harmony took them to the family room and closed the door; no one was in there thank God.

"What the fuck was that?" Harmony yelled and Bob laughed.

"See, Smurf works real well."

"You are not calling me Smurf," she said with a snap and the women laughed. "Now, someone tell me what just happened."

"Well," Shady laughed. "We all heard about how you were mistaken about what they guys said. They were talking about Lola. Then they said Fish was letting the guys have a chance at you. But Creed and Fork said they weren't wasting their time on waiting and taking a shot. They said you could turn them down and after waiting for two years they weren't given you the choice. They knew where you stood, thought they knew it two years ago, but after hearing what happened they figured you didn't need a choice cause you were pissed off and hurt enough to stay away. Then they left and we were told to be ready to welcome the newest old lady."

"I am not an old lady, they didn't ask, they didn't discuss, they didn't say anything but yell at me and then threaten to spank me," Harmony said.

"That is kinda hot," Treat sighed.

Harmony glared at her. "Yeah it was, but *that is not the point*. They didn't talk to me at all, then they tell me I am moving in here, I don't think so. I have a business and a life, and I am not fucking around with this shit."

Free laughed. "You know I love you right, Harmony, but they are bikers, and bikers aren't going to give you a choice in what they want. They want you, you want them, let it go and ride it out. We can figure out later how to get around them. Maybe some of the old ladies will come in with us and help us with them, you know, if they let us have the Bitches Charter."

"Doesn't help me in the now, I am pissed, I mean pissed the fuck off. How dare they come and grab me off the street, tell me I have to stay here, and act like we are together," Harmony said.

"Isn't that what you wanted?" Nike whispered.

The girl didn't talk much but when she did, it was always the truth.

"I did want that, like two years ago, and then they crushed me," Harmony said. "Now I want sensitive men, men who listen to what I say and what I want."

"No, you thought they crushed you, they didn't. Sensitive men are pansies," Treat pointed out.

"But I didn't know that until now, and I haven't had time to process it. Sensitive men are awesome; it is all about the woman, what she wants, and needs. They even bring you chocolate when you need it and shit. I swear, one of my guys, Jimmy, he is sensitive. He brings me chocolate when I am having a shitty day, and not the cheap stuff, the good stuff, Ghirardelli's Carmel," Harmony said and the other women gasped. "Plus wine, he always knows when I need wine. He is awesome."

"Is he gay? I mean Fork and Creed will never do anything to hurt you. They won't bring you chocolate or wine of course, I mean, what man is that tuned into women," Rain said. "They don't have it in them to be sensitive, it is like the missing link, not there, yeah they are assholes and are gonna piss you off. But trust me, these guys have waited for a long time. Hell, two years, and they aren't going to screw this up again. They are just going to do it in the funky biker man fashion that will have you pulling out your hair."

"Yes they will because they don't know me anymore. Hell, they never knew me; they only saw what they wanted to see. You saw them; they didn't even know I had been helping the club out for years. They only thought of me as a stupid little girl who hung around because she had a crush on them. Now that I am old enough, they see a woman who they think they can control. I am not that girl anymore. I want more; I want a partner, someone who is in tune with me. Like when I get home from work and am exhausted, I want someone to take care of me, rub my feet, draw me a bath, light me some candles and give me a back rub. Tonight I was wiped and what did I get, man handled on the street and thrown on the back of a bike," Harmony argued.

"You gotta give them a chance to get to know you. Did you tell them you were tired?" Shady shrugged. "Then if they fuck up, they are on their own, but I agree you gotta give them a chance, they are your dream men."

"Fuck, really, you are going there. Dream man? Tell them I was tired. Fuck my dream man would be able to read me. Like George Clooney in *Oceans Eleven*, I mean the man was so clued in," Harmony scoffed at her friend, she wasn't romantic, like at all.

"Hey, I can still be nice," Shady said. "I just would like to think of the possibility of a good guy being there for me."

"The possibility?" Treat laughed.

"Yeah, 'cause then I don't have to commit, I can just tell him he doesn't fit into the mold I want." Shady shrugged.

"And who would fit into the mold of the perfect man for you?" Bob laughed.

"Dwayne Johnson," Shady said without a pause.

"'The Rock', your perfect man is 'The Rock'?" Nike clapped. "Mine is Heath Ledger, not in the *Brokeback Mountain* movie, in *Knights Tale*, he was so fucking hot."

"Oh mine is Mel Gibson in the *Lethal Weapon* series, total bad boy," Treat said.

"Justin Long, without a doubt," Rain said softly and everyone fell silent. It took a minute and then the room burst out in laughter. "What, he was hot in *Live Free Die Hard*."

"We need a drink, and some food." Shady laughed and said, "Pizza."

"I am in," Freedom said.

"Me too," Bob laughed and the girls all walked out of the family room. They of course didn't know the guys had eyes in the room, and right then Monk was moving to tell the men what they needed to know to win Harmony over.

Chapter Seven

Last night was a bust. The girls rallied around each other and completely ignored the men and ended up all passed out together on the sectionals on the leaders' floor. Creed and Fork were annoyed, because every time they tried to talk to Harmony the girls ignored them. Tonight was going to be different, because tonight was Saturday. They knew Harmony, a lot more than she knew. They had studied her, they weren't just attracted to her two years ago, and they had planned to claim her.

She never noticed when she was hanging around the guys were paying attention. They followed her with their eyes, saw who she was talking to, then they would go and find out what she was up to. Granted, they didn't know she had been helping the whole fucking club with research, but it didn't surprise them. They knew she was smart, it was obvious, but they were going to win her over, that was their plan then and that was their plan now. She just needed to fucking slow down enough for them to do it.

Before they could get to the good stuff though, they had to deal with the trash. Creed made a call, and then Creed, Fork, Monk, Easy, and Poke left the compound in the early afternoon. They had a schedule and an envelope full of cash; it was time to get same answers.

As they rode their bikes to the edge of town, they were ready. So were their contacts. The gates to the prison opened up for them without stopping them. They pulled into the parking lot where the employees park and walked to the employee entrance.

Creed knocked three times and the door opened. "We have the cameras diverted for three hours, you have them back in three hours and we are good. You are logged in as the weekend office cleaning crew," Tim said. He was Slam's brother-in-law, and he was doing the club a favor. For payment of course, Creed wouldn't let anyone risk their family income for the club without reimbursement.

"Make sure you put that in you wife's account, say it is an inheritance," Fork said and the guy nodded and took the envelope and pointed to the door.

"Through there, knock three times, they are in the back room blindfolded with the doors locked," Tim said and Creed nodded.

They followed the directions and when they walked into the boiler room, Creed grinned. Just like they had asked. And he could see the two gangbangers were already nervous. They knew something was going on, they probably thought it was other prisoners.

"Well, boys, we need to have a little talk," Creed said and pulled off the hoods on the men's head.

"*No habla ingles.*" One of them spit on the ground.

"Huh," Monk said and looked at his friends.

"I think he is trying to say he doesn't speak English." Fork laughed.

"Didn't ask that, fucker," Monk said. "We already know you speak English. Heard you talking in your cell, yeah, I bet your bosses are gonna love hearing about that shit."

The two prisoners frowned and shrugged. One of them said, "*¡ORALE!*"

"Huh?" Monk said.

"Heard that one before, it means 'go for it'." Fork laughed.

"Right," Monk said and shook his head and looked back to the guy. "Glad we have a translator right."

The prisoners glared at him. "*CHINGADA*," one of the men spit out.

"Huh?" Monk said.

"He said 'fuck'," Fork said.

"Not fuck you? Just fuck?" Monk said.

"Yep," Fork said.

"So glad you are here, man, I coulda made a mistake with that one, 'cause if he would have told me to fuck off we would have had a problem. Him just saying fuck, that just makes him stupid," Monk said. "I know you have to speak

English though, I am pretty sure I heard a rumor somewhere."

"Hell yeah, when I heard Banger One tell his cell mate that he was going to tell the Feds all he knew, I clapped." Easy smiled.

"And Banger Two said they were going to lead the Feds to their stash of drugs," Poke said.

"It was beautiful, that conversation is going to make it to the outside before the end of the day," Easy said.

Both of the prisoners leaned back with a sneer and ignored what they were saying. Apparently they weren't afraid of someone telling their boss they were talking, that was interesting, most guys would be worried about that.

"No, brothers," Creed said and held up his hand. "We are done fucking around with these two little pissants, the threats are not working, you can see that, these guys are pros."

One of the guys smiled and lifted his chin to the other one, idiots. They really thought they were something.

"Okay, boss." Easy shrugged and pulled off his bag he was carrying over his shoulder. "Then since they like to torture people to get information out of them, let's see how they like it when we do it back. I remember every single scar on Freedom's body they gave her. I think we can get them to talking."

"But they didn't get Freedom to talk," Poke reminded him.

"I know, that is 'cause they were doing it wrong, they were in the right area for torture. But when you are messing with cutting people, the key is to cut into the muscles and not just the surface, that way the blood flows faster, because the muscles are full of blood when they are stressed. Take a finger," Easy said and reached to one of the guy's hands that were cuffed to the chair. The guys didn't have time to respond, Easy gripped it and snapped it. "See, look at how the blood is pooling at the wound."

Creed leaned over the screaming man. "Oh yeah, look at that, it *is* turning purple."

"Yeah, that's 'cause the blood is rushing to it," Easy said and then pulled out a knife and held it up to his friends. "If I were to cut it off now, the blood would shoot out like no ones business."

The man who they didn't touch was looking at them in horror and trying to move his chair away.

"Wait, *hombre*," Monk said. "Let me give this a go."

Monk reached down and grabbed one of the man's fingers who was trying to get away and snapped it. He screamed and Monk laughed. "Yeah, look at that, purple."

"Cool, guys, but we need some answers, and so let's move on to the lessons that are really going to make an impact," Fork said.

For the next hour, Easy and Poke showed the guys how to get the maximum amount of blood pooled to a joint or limb to cause the maximum amount of bleeding. Fingers, toes, knees, elbows, nothing was left untouched or unbroken on the men. They screamed and cried as Poke and Easy showed the guys the way to break a bone. But they never asked them any questions, they ignored them when they cried out they would talk.

"Cool, now that we have blood pockets all over the body," Easy said, "the fun part starts."

"Really?" Monk said. "'Cause that was pretty fun to watch, man."

"Oh yeah," Poke said. "Easy is the master of bleeding a dude out. I have seen him drain a fuckin' dude in like three minutes, never hitting the main arteries. It was slow and painful, longest three minutes of my fucking life, 'cause the screaming is terrible the whole time, up to the last second."

"Cool," Creed said and looked at Easy and nodded.

"So…" Easy said and held up the knife.

"Wait," one of the men yelled. "We are in a prison, you can't kill us in here, it is illegal."

Monk laughed and looked at Creed. "Boss, you here?"

"Nah, man, I am at the club at a party right about now," Creed said. "I got fifty people that say so."

"You will never get away with this," the other one cried. "He knows everything."

"Yeah, he who?" Fork laughed. "'Cause the only one who we are worried about is the one who is behind all this. You and your little pissant friends who think they run this place are not the head guy. He is too smart; you all have been running fast and loose with shit, making more problems for him than what he wants. I bet he expects you are gonna die."

"No, he doesn't, he can't put a hit on us or he would never…" one of them said.

"Never what?" Creed said slowly.

The man laid back and laughed. "You don't know, you still don't know, do you?"

"Easy," Creed said and pointed to the one who was laughing on the ground through his pain.

Easy nodded and ran his knife along the man's knee to where the joint was already bulging. The man screamed and his friend closed his eyes.

"Know what, asshole," Creed barked.

"What this is all about, wait, who this is all about, wait, how this all came about," the man babbled and Creed shook his head. *Fucking asshole, he was crazy.*

They turned to the silent guy and Fork kicked him in the head with his boot to make him pay attention. "What is he talking about?"

The man shook his head and Easy ran his knife along his collarbone where they had broken it. Blood poured down his chest, he screamed and they waited for both men to get themselves under control.

"Now, let's try this again. What are you talking about?" Creed said.

"I don't think they are speaking English again." Monk laughed and the others grinned.

"Fork," Creed said. "Translate for me."

"Sure," Fork nodded.

"How do you say…'listen here, muther fuckers, either you tell us what we want to know or we are going to slice and dice you, then we are going to find your family'. Monk here likes the women, he would love to show them what a real biker is like in bed. Then we will kill them like this too, it doesn't matter to us," Creed said. "Hey, maybe we should just fuckin' leave and do that now, come back later on and show them pictures, you think that would give them some incentive?"

"Shit, boss," Poke said and pulled out his phone. "I got me some pictures here already. I think this is one of your women, right?"

The man who had been kinda crazy shut up and the other one looked over. "And this one," Poke said. "This one is your sister, right, bro?" he said and showed the silent one a picture. They had already planned this.

"Yeah, that is what I thought." Easy laughed. "Glad I took the right pictures. I know right where they are today. It is Saturday, they are at the market, should be heading home soon, we can catch them together."

"Cool," Creed said and clapped his hand and leaned over. "You two don't go anywhere alright."

"Fuck," the quiet one of them swore and said, "I will tell you."

"Oh look, now they speak English, told you." Monk laughed.

"Start talking," Creed said and the two men finally gave them what little information they had. However, it was more than what they had before and it was all so clear, the Warriors hadn't even touched the tip of what was going on.

*****

The men were washing themselves up at the gas station before they went back to the compound. They had blood all over them, and they didn't want people to stare.

"You believe them?" Monk said.

"That they didn't know who was pulling the strings?" Creed said.

"Yeah," Monk said and Creed was silent and then looked at the guys.

"They would have told us. But the other stuff, man that is wacked. Torching Harmony's place like that. Someone had to tell them about her. Someone in the club, shit, I didn't even know until today she is the one who hacked the county records. How the fuck would they know?" Creed said.

"We have already checked all of our people out, man, after what happened with Trick, everyone was questioned and vetted," Monk said.

"We missed someone?" Fork said quietly.

"No way, I would have caught on to that," Easy said. "Rode a few of those guys pretty hard, there isn't any way one of the them with us right now is talking."

"What about before?" Creed said.

"Only a few guys who have moved on. One of them in the Cali Chapter, though, I could give him a call and have him come back. Two went up north to the Montana Chapter, don't know if they are still there," Monk said and Creed nodded.

"Already called the Cali Chapter, Slider is coming in next week for the party, he wanted to be here when the Savages came. We need to get a line on the others, see what they know, if they know," Creed said.

Fork nodded. "We aren't telling anyone yet that Slider is coming."

"Good, piss some people off," Monk said.

"They can talk to me if they have a problem. He is solid," Creed said.

"Diablos wanting the plans to the mine is gonna be an issue. They are planning something, and we have no clue what it is," Fork said.

"Yeah, and since those assholes say they already have an entrance on our land that only they know about? That is fucked up," Poke said.

"It would explain how Freedom's dad's head got on the grounds without us seeing anyone place it there," Easy said.

"Yeah, and if what that dude is saying is true, and they have been in and out of the compound over the last month, scoping out things, we are going to have to clear the compound to make sure they didn't fuck with anything," Poke said.

"This is gonna be a busy week, we can't let anyone know that our security isn't working. The Savages need to see us as impenetrable," Creed said.

"We also need to see who was with the club back when Harmony was looking into shit. Hang ons, whores, Prospects that didn't make it, everyone. Leave no stone unturned, because someone knows what Harmony can do, which makes her a commodity, and there is no way they are going to not realize that," Creed said.

"She stays in the compound, on the grounds, guarded at all times, not fucking around with this, Creed," Fork said.

"I hear ya," Creed said and put a hand on his neck. "But she is gonna be pissed and protest, shit, when we left this morning I was thinking about what the fuck she'd do to our bed while we were gone."

Before they left, Fork and Creed had gotten Harmony into their bed to keep sleeping, the noise of people getting up and cooking would have woken her and they both had noticed she had bags under her eyes last night when they picked her up. She needed to sleep in, so they had moved her. But they were sure she was going to be pissed when she realized whose room she was in.

Chapter Eight

She was right where she wanted to be, and if those assholes thought she was going to stay all nice and happy in the clubhouse, they were so wrong. When she had woken up and discovered where she was, Harmony had burst into action. They weren't going to put her into their bed without first working for it a little. Shit, she had more dignity than that. She knew she was going to sleep with them, she wasn't stupid.

Of course, Harmony had realized it last night when she had been dragged up to the top floor of the clubhouse and was hanging with the girls. The guys were watching them, waiting, but they had respected the fact they were ignoring them. It made them a few brownie points.

Also, she noticed Fork and Creed had watched her, when she got done with a glass of wine, they refilled it. When her plate was empty, they took it and put it in the dishwasher—it wasn't chocolate and roses, but it was something. She knew they had an ulterior motive, they wanted to talk to her, but she wasn't ready.

After hanging with the girls, and seeing the way the guys were with them in private, she was curious. Well, curious enough to sleep with Creed and Fork and see what happened. But they were going to have to work for it.

So, Shady and the other girls helped her this morning. Fish had stayed over as well, and Harmony went to her father and told him she needed space. That was all it took. He arranged for her to be put in the closest house to the clubhouse on the compound. It was right next to the shed, and usually where the overflow from the party went.

They corralled some Prospects, cleaned up the place, and sent them to her house for some clothes. Once they returned, Harmony and Shady moved in. Shady said she was staying with her until they figured shit out; she didn't like her being in the house alone. Harmony hadn't argued.

Together they organized the house, and Harmony decided she really loved the house they were in. Growing up they had lived in town in an apartment. It was home, but being in the house Harmony felt like the place could be a home. Even if it was on the compound property. It had four bedrooms on the top floor, the Warriors had redecorated it several times, but in the end, it held a master suite that Harmony had claimed as her own. The bed was fucking huge and she loved it. The bathroom held a shower ten people could fit into, but the huge bathtub was what had drawn her into the room. It was right out of a spa catalog. She was in love. All she could think of was going to the store and purchasing every single bottle of bubble bath she could find. It would take months to get her out of the bathtub if she allowed herself that luxury, so Harmony refrained.

The whole house was painted white, and Harmony could envision redecorating to make each room its own. Shady took the next largest bedroom, which also had a bathroom attached. The other two rooms had a jack and jill bathroom that was shared, although none of the rooms were tiny. There was a hidden staircase in the master suite that took you to the top floor. When Harmony and Shady had found it, they had been shocked to see a small room that could be used as an office; it was perfect. It held window seats and when they looked out, they could see the whole compound. Shady told her that she had never known about the extra floor and was surprised that none of the guys had told her. Maybe they didn't know about it.

The main floor was open. A large sunken family area with the normal sectionals the clubhouse held although these were a grey instead of black. The kitchen held stainless steel appliances, and was completely stocked. Shady explained that one of the old ladies held the job of keeping the place clean. A large dining room that held a large table, and then there was another office/den and a bathroom. All in all the place was made for a family.

"So," Shady said when they had finished making sure everything was cleaned up and were settling down into the living room to wait for the explosion, which was sure to come when Creed and Fork found out they had moved in here. "What do you think they are going to say?"

"Don't care," Harmony shrugged. "This place is perfect, I can have my business office in the den, and a personal one on the top floor where no one can bug me. If they want me to stay here, this is where I am staying. I'm not into the whole sharing the floor thing, sorry but for some reason that's kinda weird to me. Not that I care what you all do, to each his own you know. I just know myself, I would be too worried about someone seeing me naked."

Shady grinned. "You do realize what you just said right?"

"What?" Harmony laughed.

"Honey, you are giving them a chance." Shady laughed.

"Yeah well, who knows if they are gonna make the cut," Harmony grumbled.

"They will make the cut, honey," Shady laughed and Harmony rolled her eyes.

"This is just weird, you know, I have been pissed at them for so long I don't know how to let that shit go," Harmony said quietly.

"This is your chance, honey, I know they are assholes and you want to protect yourself from them again, but you gotta let someone in," Shady said.

"I let you in," Harmony said quietly.

"Yeah, but I don't want to fuck your brains out and cuddle afterwards," Shady snorted.

"They want to cuddle?" Harmony asked quietly.

"Fuck yeah they do, weird assholes." Shady laughed.

Harmony shook her head and looked at her best friend. She knew what had happened, she was one of the only ones but Shady never talked about it, she was going to have to in order to move on. She knew it and so did Harmony, but now was not the time.

They heard the guys come home before they saw them. The rumble of the bikes echoed into the house. Harmony leaned back into the couch and waited. It didn't take long.

The front door burst open, Creed and Fork stalked inside, and stopped when they saw Shady and Harmony curled up on the couches like they lived there.

"Shady," Creed said.

"Yep," her friend laughed.

"Give us a minute," Creed replied, never taking his eyes off Harmony.

Her friend chuckled and then stood. "Be in my room."

"Right," Fork mumbled and they waited for Shady to leave the room. When they heard the soft click of the door upstairs the men went to where she was sitting. Both of them sat on either side of her. She could feel their anger and frustration coming off them in waves but she was standing her ground.

"Babe," Fork said quietly.

"Listen," Harmony said, having planned all this out in her head. "I was pissed when you brought me here yesterday, pissed that you just made decisions for me without asking. It took me all night to get over being pissed about that. Because I have been taking care of my dad and myself for a long time. I am not one of those delicate flowers who needs the big strong guys to protect her. That being said, I am also not an idiot, after a few hours I realized the Diablos are up to something. I felt it yesterday and was going to talk to Monk about it. So being here is a smart move. However, being in the clubhouse is not for me. Sorry if that doesn't fit into your plans, but it is what it is. I grew up here, I know what happens here, and I am cool with it. But I need my space, I always have, if the others don't that is cool but I do. I get that two years ago I made an assumption, but looking back it was the best thing. I found myself in those two years, my father loves to tell me I have an old soul, maybe he is right, whatever. Either way I know myself, and I know that if we would have gotten together two years ago I would have lost myself because I was so wrapped up in what you wanted that I wasn't taking care of what I wanted. I woke up this morning and I was pissed, mostly because I couldn't believe you had taken another choice away from me and moved me into your bed. Then when I thought about it, I realized you were trying to be nice. I get that, but I do not nor will I ever accept when a choice is taken away from me, that isn't how I am hardwired and you need to know that. I can't be the girl who falls into line with every single thing you do or say. I won't be. So we came out here, I like it here and I like that I am comfortable here, I can see me staying here for as long as this takes."

"You done?" Creed said quietly, and Harmony nodded and took a deep breath.

"Wait no, I also am gonna add I know you are having a party this weekend, this house is the overflow, Shady explained it to me, but there is no overflow coming here, 'cause if I have to throw away another fucking condom wrapper I am gonna gag, that was just gross," Harmony finished.

"Cool," Fork said. "But that was not what Creed was asking. He meant are you done 'cause we are hungry and wondering if you wanted to order some food."

"But," Harmony said, looking back and forth between the two men wondering when the yelling was gonna start. They had been yelling at her since she had come to the clubhouse two days ago, it was their thing.

"Babe, hungry. If you are done talking we are gonna order out Chinese." Creed shrugged.

Harmony just nodded, she didn't know what to expect because they had sent Shady away when they first walked in. She had expected a throw down of epic proportions, and with them giving in and not demanding that she conform to their wishes, was strange and unsettling. Fork stood and went to the kitchen to grab the phone. Creed sat next to her relaxed and leaning backwards into the couch.

"Two men," Creed said.

"Huh?" Harmony said, why were they always speaking in code with her.

"Two men have to guard the house at all times," Creed said. "This is not open for discussion. When Fork and I are not in the house, two of the Prospects will be on guard. When we are here, they go away. Fork and I will be moving our shit over in a while. We'll take the two bedrooms that are open until you are ready to open your room to us. We can negotiate on space for office shit, but Fork and I will need at least a desk for computers. The den is big, we shouldn't have a problem there, but we may need to look at adding on a room though because we need to have some privacy to deal with club shit, and you need to deal with your business. We can work that shit all out though. Now you still like General Tao's Chicken or have your taste buds changed in the last two years?"

Harmony stared at Creed like he had grown a second head, who was this calm person sitting in front of her. And how the hell did he know what she ordered every single time they got Chinese.

"Babe?" Fork said covering the phone. "General Tao's?"

Harmony nodded and just sat back, she had no idea where to go with this—it was weird. Creed picked up the remote to the television and then yelled at Shady to come back down. Her best friend was grinning when her feet hit the bottom step and she saw Creed and her sitting next to each other on the couch and Fork ordering food for them on the phone. When Fork was done, he plopped back down next to her and flopped an arm over the back of the couch behind her. Shady sat across from them, grinning from ear to ear. Harmony could literally feel the tides changing in the room, she just didn't know how they had done it. Arrogant bastards.

*****

"You two wanna tell me why all of a sudden you want to have a ladies club?" Creed said while they were eating.

Shady looked at Harmony and she shrugged, maybe if they talked to him about it he would come around before presenting it to the club.

"Look," Shady said and leaned back. "We aren't the usual women who hang around a club. I get that you have the old ladies and the whores, I get the hang ons are pussy for the guys, but some of us are not like that and you know it."

Creed nodded and Fork said, "You aren't and we never have treated you like that because we know you aren't."

Shady nodded. "I know, just saying. But lately I have been thinking about shit, especially when it came to Trick."

"Shay," Creed said softly. "That was fucked up, I mean seriously fucked up, not something I would usually ask you to do."

"I know," Shady said again and shrugged. "That wasn't my point. My point was, shit like that sometimes needs to be done. I get it, Free gets it, hell, even Harmony gets it and she wasn't here, but I told her about it afterwards because it was messing with my head a little."

Creed and Fork both looked surprised that Shady would talk to someone outside the club about club shit. They had never talked about it with her before because they figured she was dealing with it with Free. "Shady, you know you can't."

"Save it," Shady held up her hand. "I didn't go broadcasting it around town or anything. I said we talked about it, and we did. Harmony is my sounding board, has been for a long time. She would never betray the club. That is just an example though of shit. I couldn't come to one of you because you are guys. Sometimes though the girls need to talk, we can't go to the outside so we need to be able to talk to each other. You guys know what is said in church stays in church, well I think the same goes for us. Sometimes we need to blow off some steam and we need to know we can do that without it all coming back to bite us in the ass. We do a lot of shit for the club, the Shop, books that Free has taken over. Let's face it, we are part of the club but because women will never be full members, we need to feel like we matter still. Having the Warrior Bitches will give us that."

"How are you planning to set it up?" Fork asked, almost like it was a forgone conclusion they would be allowed to set up the female charter.

"Same as you guys, minus the enforcers, I figure we have you all for that. We don't need any butch chicks to be standing guard and shit. That isn't what this is about, it is about taking care of business—our business," Shady said.

"So you gonna be Prez?" Creed said and looked at Shady closely who was mulling it around in her head.

"I don't know," Shady said honestly. "I never thought of myself as a leader but the last few months I can see that is the role I have taken on. With Free and all the shit that went down with her it seemed natural that I stepped up. Now I don't know if I want all that, but I do know I want to be part of the leadership. Free too, I know she does and I think she is a good balance to my bitchiness, she is sweet. I don't do sweet. Bob and Nike, they are happy to follow along. Rain and Treat, I see them as wanting to be part of the leadership, nothing huge but they have been here for a long time and they have always had my back."

"What about Harmony?" Fork said and looked at her. She had been just listening to them talk, making sure she could see both sides of things. It was how she worked and so she was silent while they stared at her. She had to think it over for a second before she spoke.

"I want to be a part of the leadership," she said finally. Creed and Fork nodded and smiled at her. They looked so proud, she felt like she had gotten an award.

"I think that you three woman would be awesome leaders in the club. Write it up and let me make sure everyone is cool with it and then we will let you know. But if I explain it like you just did, I don't think they will have a problem with that at all. I am pretty sure this is gonna fly because they respect you and the other girls," Creed said and Shady nodded and turned back to the television, apparently the conversation was over.

Harmony shifted, she was still in between the two men, and she was feeling their closeness. Damn it, being near them made her want to take them upstairs and progress this relationship, but they weren't there yet. She knew if she gave into them, they would try to run over her. So she ignored the heat between her legs.

Chapter Nine

Lola picked up the phone and made the call she had been waiting to make for years. She knew Creed and Fork wanted that little bitch, but they were never going to have her. It didn't matter what she had to do, Harmony was never going to be their old lady.

She had work and slaved for years to try to get their attention. It had worked for a short time, everything seemed to be in her grasp, and then Harmony grew up. What the fuck was so special about her? Nothing, other than the fact she had been the one to do the research of the mines.

Dom had contacted her looking for his sister, she was one of the Bitches, and he had seen her around town with the guys. Lola had jumped on the chance to help him, anything to take the competition away. There was too much of it, Shady with her hand in everything, Nike with her sweet innocent act, and of course then there was Harmony, the little princess, bitch needed to be smacked down and put in her place.

As soon as she heard who Dom was looking for and why, she had been thrilled. It would kill two birds with one stone, but it backfired. She was the one who was kicked out of the club, *fucking assholes*. She had to team up with Dom because he had good connections. Well this time their plan was foolproof and she wanted it all, shit, she deserved it. Laying on her back for the last two years for Dom, she deserved a medal and more—he was one sick fuck.

It was simple; they were going to run the clubs out of the two towns they had picked to be the main hub for distribution for the cartel. Then they would have the mine and the pipeline bringing them money. Of course, the cartel knew nothing of the mine and they weren't telling them; that was for her and Dom to split, they had an agreement. First things first though, the clubs weren't going to leave just because they were hassling them. No, they needed a good fucking reason to leave, and Lola was going to give them one.

"The dancers have their meetings at the first of every week, going over who gets what station for the week, and unless it has changed, that's on Mondays. Scout it out, and if it is then we will hit the following week," Lola said. "Don't worry, I will have her there, I have something she is going to want to look at."

*****

They were moving shit into the house, *her house*, Harmony thought. Of course, they had said they were going to but to be honest, she really thought they were talking about a bag of clothes and a few laptops and that was it. Fuck no; those bastards hadn't informed her they were seriously moving everything from the clubhouse to this house.

After she had woken up this morning, went down and made breakfast in the amazing kitchen, sat, and drank coffee on the back porch as the sun rose over the hills of the mine—she had been in heaven. She loved this house and began to think she could talk to her father into claiming this as theirs so they could move out here instead of being in town. Then she could get used to being out here, get to know everyone again, and basically get used to being with the club again. Apparently, Creed and Fork weren't going to let her do this though because both of those bastards were running over her again.

All of their shit, down to the sheets and blankets from the clubhouse, were being moved over here. Shit, she even saw a fucking jock strap hanging out of a bag, who the fuck wore jock straps anymore?

She stood in her bedroom looking down as the men were moving more and more stuff into her house—it was hers, she had decided and damn it they were so not going to take it from her. The rage in her was building, it didn't make sense, it didn't have to, fucking A she was PMSing, and they were fucking up her plans for her life.

Then she saw them, the banes of her existence, and she lost any reason she had been holding onto. Stomping to her dresser, she pulled out her gun she had brought to her yesterday. She checked the bullets and grinned when she saw she had a full clip. This was the first gun she had ever bought. Monk had taken her to the gun store and stood with her while she had been like a kid in a candy shop, they had all been amazing but the Beretta had caught her eye. Usually not for women, Harmony had scoffed at the dealer and asked if she could try it out in the small range he had attached to the store. The man had reluctantly agreed and that was only after Monk had convinced him he would take full responsibility if she shot her foot off. She had been sold on it right away. It was a little heavy for her hand, but she practiced and practiced every day until it no longer felt too much for her. She loved it, she had other guns, four to be precise—although who was counting—and they all had names. Harmony's men liked to tease her about it, but she had seen it in a movie once, a guy naming his gun, and she had loved it.

   When Monk was teaching her, he explained the relationship most owners had with their guns if they were serious about it. It was personal, and she took it seriously and so she named her gun. 'Shirley' had saved her more times than she could count over the last two years. Well not more times than she could count, that may be an exaggeration, but more than on one hand, so she felt a connection with the gun. When she used it to save her life when a crack addict mistakenly thought she was a sandwich from Subway and was trying to eat her, seriously, he actually took her arm and tried to eat it, she had shot him in the foot. Made a statement and saved her from being zombiefied.

   Harmony stomped back over to the window and glared down, *first rule of owning a gun, never use your weapon in anger, fuck that*. She opened her window and grinned because Creed and Fork were thanking the guys for helping as they were leaning against Creed's brand new truck he used for going to the mine. His Harley didn't like the rough dirt roads.

"Hey," Harmony yelled down and the men looked up at her. "I thought you were only moving in for a short time, what the fuck is all this?"

Creed grinned up at her and said, "Babe, never said a short time, you are here, and so we are here. You move somewhere else, we move somewhere else. What part of we are claiming you as our old lady did you not understand?"

"The part where you were claiming me as your old lady. I haven't made up my mind about that," Harmony yelled and Creed laughed.

No shit, he actually laughed. She really was beginning to wonder what the hell she had ever saw in him and Fork. They were making her question her own damn sanity. They didn't listen to a thing she said, only what they expected her to say. Well, they were in for a rude awakening, the railroading assholes.

"Babe," Fork said as he shook his head up at her. "You made up your mind the second you walked back in the gate."

"No I didn't, you pissed me off, and I was coming here to yell at you," Harmony said.

"Could have used the phone, babe," Fork said.

"Spoon, when your place is fire bombed and you are pissed off because it wasn't your fault but you knew whose fault it was, you can come and talk to me about how you would react. Until then, shut the fuck up," Harmony yelled. "This is my house, my place to live while shit is going down, my place to get my shit together and decide if I want to give you a chance."

"You made you choice, and I am telling you, call me Spoon one more time and I am spanking that ass raw," Fork yelled.

"I don't want you here," she screamed.

"Yes you do," Creed laughed and she almost lost her mind. "If you didn't, you wouldn't be arguing so much with us, you want us so much it hurts, babe, and as soon as you give us the green light we will solve your bitchiness. A few good fuckings and it should mellow you right on out."

"Yeah," Fork agreed, "and if you don't, we will tie you to the bed until it does, makes no difference to us."

"You did not just say that to me!" she screeched. "How is this for a fucking hint?"

Harmony raised her gun and pointed it at the two men who suddenly stood up straighter but didn't move a muscle like most men would have. They did not duck, they did not turn, the only thing the both of them did almost at the same time, they raised an eyebrow at her.

"Babe, not fucking funny," Fork growled.

"Yeah, well I don't think you moving into my house is funny either," Harmony yelled.

"Harmony, put that thing away right the fuck now," Creed said quietly and Harmony narrowed her eyes.

"No," she hissed. "You need to give me some space."

"YO, BOITCH!" Shady yelled from behind her and Harmony jumped, accidently squeezing the trigger. "FUCK ME!" Shady screamed again and Harmony fired once more.

Harmony closed her eyes and then looked over her shoulder and said to Shady, "Shit, Shay, don't scare a woman with a gun."

"How the fuck was I supposed to know you had a goddamn gun," Shady yelled.

Harmony looked back down to the ground and both of the men had moved, not far, just enough to bend over and look at the back tire of the brand new Dually that Creed had picked up just two days ago.

"Woman," Creed yelled as he stood. "You shot my fucking brand new truck."

Fork stood, looked at her incredulously, and yelled, "It is a Dually."

"I didn't shoot the truck, I shot the tire, and they can be replaced, drama king," Harmony snapped and Creed and Fork narrowed their eyes. Within a few seconds, they began to barrel into the house. She knew right where they were headed and with a screech, she dropped 'Shirley' on her bed and ran for it.

Shady yelled, "Going to town, have fun y'all."

"Take a Prospect," Harmony heard Creed yell as they thumped up the stairs.

She made it to the door to the top floor, slammed it, locked the door, and ran up the stairs.

"Harmony!" Fork yelled and pounded on the door.

She let out a nervous giggle and looked around. They had moved her stuff up here already, so there was a couch and desk already in place. She backed slowly to the couch and sat down on the edge, bouncing her legs up and down nervously. *Shit, they were pissed.*

"Open the fucking door, babe," Creed yelled and the pounding continued.

"No, I will wait for you to stop being pissed off," she called back.

"Not a good plan, Harmony, gonna be pissed about this for a while," Fork yelled and she heard the wood on the door crack. Fuck, they were going to break down her door.

"Hey, do not..." she yelled right when the door gave and she heard the thumping on the stairs. She panicked and stood ready to go out the window and down the drain pipe if need be, of course she didn't make it to the window, no, they caught her after three steps and she was tossed in the air over Creed's shoulder.

"YOU ASSHOLES!" Harmony yelled as he walked to the couch and pulled her off his shoulder, and sat down laying her right over his lap with her ass in the air. She was wearing a skirt and they pulled it up and over her hips so they were staring at her sexy underwear. Of course, she had worn them this morning, she had been thinking about them when she put them on, *fuck.*

"Asshole?" Creed roared. "Woman, you pointed a gun at me! Shot my truck, and fucking sassed me for the last fuckin' time."

Fork stepped right into her line of vision and said, "When he is done, I am up, calling me Spoon, being a bitch. I am gonna spank you then fuck you and not even care if you like it."

"WHAT!" she yelled and began to squirm.

"Fine, I will care if you like it and you are gonna like it cause you are fucking hot for us and I am sick of playing this goddamn game with you," Fork roared.

She felt the first slap from Creed's hand come down on her ass and she screamed. *Shit that hurt*, she thought and moved. The second time it was worse, and the third and then it changed. She could feel the heat coming from her ass and it travelled to her pussy, making it tingle. *What the fuck?* she thought and tried to get away.

Fork held her back in place while Creed continued to spank her and count aloud. "Five," smack, "six," smack, "seven," *shit, she was actually liking this*, "eight," smack, "nine," smack, "ten." Then they swapped. Fork was spanking her and she moaned a little. Her ass was on fire, her nipples were tingling, and straining against her bra, she could feel them as her chest brushed against Fork's leg. Heat swept through her as she took their punishment.

When they reached five, Creed pulled her panties down and off her legs.

"Nice and pink," Creed muttered and then Fork made a noise.

"Gonna be red," Fork said and Creed laughed.

Five more and Harmony was panting on Fork's lap, she felt her arousal, her thighs coated with her juices weeping out of her cunt. Fuck, she had never been this turned on. Only a few sexual experiences and they had been with nice guys. Creed and Fork were far from nice, they were rough and tough and fuckin' sexy as hell.

"Shit, my cock is so fucking hard right now," Fork moaned and pulled her up until she was straddling his waist. She looked at his flushed face and knew her expression had to mirror his. Passion, raw, electric, fuck she could feel it pulsing through the fucking air.

"Get her undressed," Creed snapped and pulled on her t-shirt. It was off her body in the blink of an eye. She continued to stare into Fork's eyes as he looked at her breasts. He licked his lips and when she felt Creed unsnap her bra, she didn't hesitant to throw it off.

"Jesus," Fork swore. "Fucking perfect."

He bent his head and attacked her breasts. Harmony had only made noises of desire up until this point but when she felt his lips on her nipples, she cried out.

"Yes, oh damn, please," she said.

Fork leaned back so she was laying on top, still straddling his legs. Creed kicked his friend's foot and she felt him spread, in turn spreading her wide. Creed picked her up by the hips so she was on her knees with her ass in the air.

"Fuck yeah. She is fucking soaked. Our babe liked her punishment. Her cunt is weeping for us. Do you want our cocks, babe?" Creed said and Harmony nodded her head. "Words, babe."

"Fuck yes," she cried out.

Fork released her long enough to pull his shirt over his head. She grinned and ran her hands down his sculpted broad chest. She heard Creed rustling in back of her and knew he was getting undressed, and if she wasn't so fucking turned on, she would have turned her head to watch but she couldn't, she was more interested in making Fork get back to sucking her tits.

Harmony grasped her breasts and held them out for Fork, he grinned and looked at her and then devoured each of the straining tips as if he was a starving man and she was his last meal. *Shit, his mouth was heaven.* Creed turned her head, bent over, and kissed her.

Harmony moaned into his mouth, as he tasted her passion. His tongue, showing no mercy, swept into her mouth and touched every inch she would allow him to, which was all of it. Slow, deep, hard—and complete. That is how Creed kissed, a woman would know if he owned her because of the brand he put on her lips.

She felt a hand on her ass. Moving and pulling her up so she was well above Fork's lap. Creed traced a finger down her ass and plunged into her cunt without any warning. Harmony gasped and tried to pull her mouth away but Creed wouldn't let her. He owned her, and she was going to know it by the end of the afternoon.

Creed wrapped a hand in her hair and held her still, as he plundered and ravaged her mouth. Shit, she couldn't catch a breath because of the feel of Fork on her breast, nipping and pinching both nipples with his mouth and his hands, and Creed working her mouth and her cunt, shit, she was a jumbling mess.

Creed pulled his hand back and circled her asshole. *Shit*, she thought and then Fork put his hand between her legs and inserted two fingers in her roughly. She moved and moaned, riding his fingers while pushing back toward Creed's, letting them know she was feeling out of control. She had been fucked in the ass before, but he had been gentle—she didn't want gentle right now. She wanted them as out of control as she was.

"Fuck, Fork, she wants it," Creed whispered against her lips when he finally released her mouth. She was panting against him. "Tell him, tell him you want us to fuck this cunt and ass at the same time. You want to be our bitch; you want to let us fuck you, hard, fast. You want it. Tell him."

"Shit," Harmony whispered. "I want it."

"What do you want?" Creed demanded.

"You, fucker," Harmony screamed. "I want you in my ass and in my cunt and fucking me so hard I can't fucking see straight, is that so much to ask for?"

Fork chuckled. "No, babe, just checking."

"Bastards," Harmony muttered and then pushed back against Creed's hand again.

"Yeah, gonna open you wide, babe," Creed said and she felt him put one finger in her while Fork pushed his two back into her cunt. Shit, she could feel them both and she cried out. Fork grabbed her hair with his free hand, pulled her down, and began to kiss her.

They stretched her, pushed her and yes, fucking demanded her to give them her body and she did, she gave it to them with a fucking scream of frustration when they pulled away from her when she was about to come just from their hands. Then they did it again until she was ready to go and get the gun and finish them if they didn't fuck her. She voiced all of this while they laughed and her; it pissed her off and turned her on at the same time.

Somehow they rid themselves of all their clothes while they were teasing her, she didn't know how, well, she did cause she demanded it, even went so far as to push down

Fork's jeans impatiently as she stood briefly and bent over with Creed's finger in her ass. But she didn't care; all she cared about was getting their cocks in her. When she had settled back down, she grinned at Fork.

"Fuck me," she growled and demanded and Fork laughed.

"Condom," he said and Creed threw one over her shoulder. "Put it on me, babe, and make sure you give him some attention too while you are working it on."

Harmony grinned, she had seen their cocks and knew they were big, she had seen them six years ago when they had been skinny dipping with that whore, Lola. It was the only time she had gotten a piece of them and she knew it, it had broken her heart, but she had been seventeen then. Then she had been shocked, after seeing a man's cock who was considerably smaller and not nearly as long as she had craved it. Now she had them and she was going to love it.

They were no doubt the best looking men she had ever seen. Fork with his black hair and slate grey eyes that reflected almost a silver when he focused them on her. And Creed whose black hair was offset with the bluest eyes she had ever come across. Both men stood at least six foot three and the day she had seen them skinny dipping, she remember the intake of her breath when she saw their well defined sculptured bodies, covered in tats. They were hot then, but now they were smoking hot. Nothing had changed, they had only gotten better.

She wrapped her hand around Fork's cock and he moaned. Her fingers barely made it around the monster and she grinned. *Yep, they were going to split her in two*, she thought.

She pumped it a few times, then ran her finger over its tip, and wiped the small bead of come that was already leaking. Fascinated with what she as doing, she didn't realize until Creed tapped his cock to her cheek that she had been licking her lips, apparently ,they had noticed though because Creed was offering her a taste of him before he buried himself in her ass. She grinned bigger and opened her mouth.

Creed grabbed the back of her hair and held on as he fucked her face. Fork grasped her hand and held it around hers as she pumped his cock in the same rhythm. *Shit, they were fucking hot.* They were using her for their pleasure and she was happy to fuckin' let them—this time. Next, she wanted one of them to eat her out because she had heard stories about their mouths and she wanted some of that.

"Shit," Creed said. "Enough, I wanna come in that fucking ass."

Harmony nodded and then turned and put Fork's condom on his cock. She wasted no time in getting him ready and he was laughing at her impatience.

"I think her cunt is lonely, buddy," Fork said.

"Yeah, well not for long, her ass is still red and begging to be reamed, I would guess the same for her cunt, fill her up, man," Creed laughed and she moaned from their dirty talk.

She lifted herself until she was positioned over Fork's cock, then slowly began to lower herself on him, savoring the feel of her pussy sliding over him. But he wasn't having any of that, she needed a lesson and slow could come later, now she needed to feel them slamming into her, if they were lucky she wouldn't sit for a week when they were done with her.

He pushed up and pulled her down at the same time, stretching her pussy for the first time in about a year. Shit, she should have prepared herself with a bigger dildo. If she had known, she would have because Fork was fucking huge, and Creed was just as big. When she felt him pressing into her ass, she threw back her head and made a noise that no one would say was normal, it was raw and guttural and she was fucking feeling it.

Fork stayed still as Creed pushed into her ass. She was so fucking full, and she screamed because it felt so amazing.

"DON'T FUCKIN' STOP!" she yelled and both men chuckled.

"Don't worry, babe, gonna fuck you raw," Creed whispered in her ear and she shivered.

They both entered her, filling her, Harmony could feel every pulse inside her, and she closed her eyes. This was heaven, this is what she was made for—them. Finally, she had enough and begged them to start moving.

"Please," she whispered. "Please!" she said louder. "Fucking move."

They complied and began to fuck her; one pulling out while the other pushed in, over and over, creating a friction in her cunt and ass that completely drove her out of her mind.

So good.

Fork reached between them and began to tease her clit while they fucked her. It set her off in a way she had never been set off before. It was like fire, her body had a mind of its own, chasing the explosion she new was coming.

"Fuck, babe," Fork moaned. "Squeezing the life out of my cock. Your pussy is like fucking heaven."

"So is her ass, like a glove made for me," Creed said and then moved faster and faster until she was thrashing in their arms completely out of control.

With a scream Harmony burst apart, coming so hard, she shook with the passion, and both of the men followed her close behind. As they panted and tried to regain some sort of thought, the only sounds in the room were their breaths.

"Knew it would be good but fuck, babe, you almost killed us," Creed said, pulling out slowly.

"Fuck yeah, what a way to go though." Fork laughed from under her, his head leaned back against the couch with his eyes closed. Harmony curled into his chest and snuggled.

"Am I outta trouble?" she mumbled.

"Fuck no," Creed laughed. "That only bought you a reprieve for a few hours. By the end of the night you will need five days to fucking recover."

"Oh good," Harmony said. "I thought that was all."

"What?" Fork roared and then sat up and looked at her. She smiled and shook her head.

"You are so easy." She laughed and they set about making good on their threat.

Chapter Ten

"Oh my God," Harmony said into the pillow, moaning from the aches in her body.

"You hurting, babe?" Fork said against her back and she shivered. She remembered last night, all night, the two men who were sharing her bed, taking her repeatedly until they had fallen into an exhausted sleep. They hadn't even eaten dinner, fucking their way through the day. Never had she seen any man who could recover as fast as these two. She'd lost count of the condoms used and then began to wonder where they were getting them from. If they kept up like that, they were either going to have to stop using them, or buy stock in them.

One phone call from Easy and Creed informed them not to disturb them again, and to tell Shady to spend the night in the compound. His enforcer had laughed and said he would take care of it.

"Every muscle in my body hurts," she moaned and Creed chuckled.

"You know they say if you are sore you should just fuck again and it would loosen you up."

"Are you kidding me?" she moaned.

"Hey, I got morning wood and Fork isn't allowed anywhere near my cock," Creed said.

Harmony laughed loudly. "Good to know I won't have any competition."

"Sorry, babe, I have a tat on my ass that says 'exit only'," Fork said and she snorted.

"How did you guys decided to do this, share a women?" she asked finally. She had been wanting to know.

"Well," Creed said and rolled over so he was facing her. Fork moved so he was laying on his back and cuddling her a little. "We grew up together. Fork's parents were fucked up, mom and dad both trying to play games putting him in the middle, and then one day his dad took it too far. Beat Fork with a fucking belt until he passed out. Fork called me, I called my dad, and my dad went and got him. Brought him back to the compound, he was fifteen and a mess. We waited for his parents to send the cops out here to get him because my father had created a fucking mess by beating the shit out of his dad and locking his mom in a closet to get to Fork. But no one came. My dad told him he had a place here and here he stayed. We went to school together, we were in the club together, prospected together, and went in the military together. Been together since we were fifteen. When we were in the military, had leave and went to a whorehouse, we shared our first woman and from there on out we knew what we liked. But we never thought we would ever find a woman who would be able to handle us for a lifetime. We saw you, knew you were the one, and then you froze us out. Easy and Poke met Free, we figured maybe we would get another chance, and then you showed up. From the first second you stepped back on this land you were ours, we decided the night you froze us out if we got a second chance with you, we wouldn't waste it, and we didn't."

Harmony felt the tears gathering in her eyes, damn it, why did they have to do sweet now? She needed asshole, not sweet.

"I am sorry about your parents," she whispered to Fork who smiled against her shoulder.

"Babe, long time ago, I am over it. What is jacked though is that I have a half brother that didn't fair as well as me. My mom screwed around on his dad and came up pregnant with me. His dad was a fucking bastard and refused to raise me but wouldn't let her take him. Our mom got with my dad who hid his assholishness, well, at least for a while. Didn't find out until later that my dad had his dad thrown out on the street, ruined him, made sure the guy had nothing to provide my brother with. It was shit, still is shit, because he grew up hating me and I grew up hating him because I took all of the beatings from my father every time they fought it always came back to her causing all the problems because she couldn't keep her legs closed. My mom refused to fucking stand up for him or me. Allowed my dad to just take his pain out on me," Fork muttered.

"You have a brother?" Harmony said and Fork nodded slowly.

"Yeah, babe, you gotta know who though, because this weekend shit is gonna happen and not all of it good. Gotta lay this aside and get over it. That pain is in the past," Fork said.

"Why this weekend, I don't get it," Harmony said, turning a little.

Creed leaned closer and shook his head. "Harmony, Fork's brother is Tonto, Savages MC Prez."

"Fuck a duck," she whispered.

"Yeah," Fork said.

"*That's* what the hate between the two clubs is all about?" Harmony asked.

"Mostly. Tonto blames me for his shitty life, his dad's shitty life. Said I had it sweet, but he won't stand still long enough to talk to me'" Fork said.

"So we make him," Harmony said. "Family is family."

"Yeah, babe, family is family," Fork whispered. "Let's get you cleaned up."

"I am kinda squishy," she laughed.

"New word for it, babe." Creed laughed.

"Suck it up," Harmony growled.

"Morning conversation over with," Creed said and slapped her ass and she moaned. She heard him walk to the door. "Hurry up, I will be back in a few for a shower, gonna go start coffee."

"Hot shower, coffee, yeeesssss," she groaned.

"Hop to it," Fork ordered over his shoulder and walked into the bathroom.

"Turn it on, get it warm, I will be in there in a minute," Harmony moaned and tried to move.

It took her five minutes to stand and then she stumbled into the bathroom.

*****

"Guys, it's okay. I'm on birth control. You're fine. Honestly. Stop worrying." She turned to look at Fork who then smirked at her, they had taken a shower together and in the middle of it Fork decided to have the conversation with her about going bareback. Apparently, in the shower, he didn't want to suit up and he was hard for her. So when Creed came back into the room and they were drying off, Fork announced they needed to have the birth control talk 'cause he wanted nothing between them.

"Why, did you have some ideas?" She wiggled her ass against Fork's erection as it came up to play. She was giggling when Creed narrowed his eyes at her then grinned.

"I thought you were sore?" Creed said. "'Cause if I am wrong, I wasted time starting coffee, we are gonna be here for a while."

"And for your information with you, Harmony, he is always up and ready to play, but this time, you are gonna have to do all the work, you fucking wore my ass out last night." Fork picked her up only to pass her like a piece of baggage to Creed who whipped the towel off her body and then threw it on the floor.

He carried her into the bed, she loved this bed, and she thought, *whoever had thought a huge California King in this house was a good idea so needed a basket of fruit; it was perfect for them.* Although if she was honest about it, when she first saw the bed that is exactly what she had been thinking and hoping would happen.

During the early morning as she had been laying on the bed, before she tried to move, she had wondered if it was a dream. For so long she had dreamt of waking up with both of these amazing men surrounding her. And this morning it had been, she cherished it, because even though they said they wanted her, she didn't trust it yet, she couldn't. Harmony didn't trust easily, even as a child she didn't, her mother left her, and even though her father was the best dad in the world, she had known she hadn't been enough for her mother to stay. Then when she overheard what she had assumed was a conversation about her, she had been crushed. Finding out that she had been mistaken hadn't lessened the pain she felt, it had only pushed it to the side. Mostly because Harmony didn't think these alpha men were going to stick with her when they found out what she was really like, why would they? She wasn't compliant, she wasn't Betty Crocker, and she was definitely not Suzie homemaker. She was a slightly neurotic, gun toting, bitch slapping badass whose best friend was a killer. Not the kind of chick most men wanted to settle down with.

Creed apparently noticed her distraction, tossed her up in his arms, and then caught her. She laughed when Creed laid her down on the bed and ran his tongue down her body before he stood. She watched with lust filled eyes as she got a good look at both men's cocks for the first time side by side.

Goddamn, her men got touched by the cock fairy, she thought, there was no other explanation how two guys had such perfect packages. Shit, if she put all the guys she had fucked, which was only about five, next to these two, they would have run home crying in embarrassment.

Her mouth watered and she could think of nothing but wanting a taste of both men. Getting up, she looked at them both so they knew what she was going to do when she stood in front of them before sinking to her knees. Reaching out, she grabbed both men's dicks and pumped them back and forth before she leaned over and swirled the head of Fork's erection with her tongue allowing the drop of pre-cum to leak out giving her the first taste of him. He was salty, but it made her crave more. Sucking him in her mouth she grabbed him around the base and pumped the thick shaft, which she almost couldn't fit in her mouth. Not wanting to leave Creed out, she released Fork and did the same to Creed's cock. Both men seemed to groan with each pass she made. Sucking them in and out, tasting each of them.

"Enough," Fork commanded before lifting her up and throwing her on the bed, but instead of falling on top of her, he spread her thighs, burying his face between her legs, causing her to cry out as he pushed his finger inside her cunt.

Creed took the moment to get on the side of her, sucking her breast into his mouth. Shit, his mouth was fucking amazing, she was going to have bruises on her tits because of the amount of play they had gotten in the last twenty-four hours. But she didn't care, she would walk around like a cowgirl who had been rode hard and put up wet for the sensations they were giving her.

Fork ate her pussy like a champion, making sure she felt each pass of his finger and flick of his tongue on her clit. She had set something off in him yesterday, and he and Creed weren't going to let her go now. She was there and it was time she knew and accepted it—their fucking old lady, that's what she was.

Flipping her over, he positioned himself at her opening and gently pushed all the way inside until he was balls deep. Creed moved in front of her quickly and she automatically grabbed his cock, sucking him down. She swallowed around his thick cock and was rewarded with a moan. Creed gripped the back of her hair and held her in place.

"Fuck," he swore. "Gonna fuck your face, babe, take it all, everything I am giving you."

Harmony moaned around his cock in agreement. She couldn't wait, this time one of them were coming in her mouth. She felt the power, it was what she needed right then.

Fork kept his momentum slow and steady, enjoying the feel of her pussy around his dick. She was hot and tight, and it was pure heaven. He could stay inside her forever. He watched as she hollowed her cheeks, sucking Creed down with earnest and his friend grunted and groaned with each pass. He knew what her mouth felt like, a hot furnace that could drive a man insane.

He picked up the rhythm a little as he collected the juices that flowed and took his thumb, playing with her asshole. Harmony grinned inside, they loved her ass, and she had to say she had been surprised at her feelings on it as well. It had not been her favorite position before but damn it ranked right up there with the two men's cocks. *Shit, she would be feeling like she had something up her ass for days*, she mused.

She began to get excited, tightening her lips around Creed's cock, she wanted them to come together, shooting inside her at the same time. Fork continued to play and push inside her until he hit the sweet spot in her ass. Whatever he did, it set her off because she hummed and it set Creed off as he called out her name, increasing his speed.

Harmony waited until they were pounding into her to use all her muscles in her mouth and pussy to squeeze them at the same time. She wanted to make them crazy, and she succeeded. Fork pounded in her fast, and Creed used two hands to hold her head as he moved, *shit, this was nuts*.

"Fuck, I can't last much longer, help push her over." Fork seemed to know what she needed, he reached between her legs and started to rub her clit. Fork removed his finger from her ass and grabbed her hip to hold her steady. Within seconds, she screamed around Creed's cock as they both emptied deep inside her.

Quickly rolling to the side, Fork pulled her with him as Creed pulled his now soft cock out of her mouth. He left the room only to come back with two warm cloths. He threw one at Fork and then cleaned her face and her pussy then wiped himself clean as well before tossing it in the hamper in the corner of the room.

"I say we take a nap and then deal with the world. Mmm, okay?" Harmony said half dazed as she rolled over and rested her head on Fork's chest. Creed joined them in the bed and pulled the blankets over the three of them, soon they all fell to sleep.

Creeds last thought before he dozed off, *she was made for us.*

*****

Five days it took to get everything moved and ready for the party at the compound. It also took her two days to recoup before her men decided she was fully ready to take them again. Of course, according to Fork, they were fucking the attitude out of her because in those five days she had been just as sassy with them as she had been previously.

One thing Harmony found was that punishments were fun, so she set out to piss them off as many times as she could, because she always ended up the winner. Happy and sedated in bed as they tried to tame her. It didn't work.

They found this out when one of the Prospects refused to let one of her men in the gate. It had been a race to catch her as she grabbed her gun and took off for the front gate.

"Babe," Fork called as he ran after her laughing.

"No," Harmony called over her shoulder, never slowing her pace. "You said my guys would have access to the compound for assignments and meetings. This is the third fucking time one of those idiots has refused to open the gate."

Creed had jumped on his bike, wanting to make sure he caught her before there was bloodshed. As he roared up next to her, he smiled at her.

"Can't let you shoot our Prospects," Creed said to her.

"Fuck that," Harmony stormed. "You can get a new one, he isn't patched in yet."

"Still can't let you do that." Creed laughed.

"I have a job, I have a company, and it doesn't work unless my guys have access to me. We talked about this, it isn't funny. Jimmy is bringing seriously important Intel to me about the Diablos. I found a trail, I told you that, he followed it, we need to know what they are up to," Harmony yelled and then reached the curve right before the gate and she could see the Prospect standing with his arms folded in front of her man denying him access still.

Fork yelled as he drew up next to her because she had slowed down a little. She was fast, she knew it, and Fork had been in his biker boots, no competition next to her high tops.

"Prospect, back the fuck off."

The young guy turned and his eyes got wide as he took in a very pissed off Harmony pointing her Beretta at him. "Shit," he yelled and moved quickly.

Harmony laughed and followed him with her arm. "Listen here, you fucker, when one of my guys comes to the gate and says he needs to fucking talk to me you let him in."

"Shit," the Prospect yelled and Jimmy laughed and shook his head and went back to his car and got in, ready to drive up to the house. Fork ran forward and pushed the button to open the gates and Jimmy drove through as Harmony followed the young man with her gun as he ran to get away.

"Babe," Creed laughed. "Put the fucking gun down."

"No, he needs a lesson," Harmony growled and Jimmy pulled up next to her, leaned over, and looked up.

"Hey, boss, got the papers." Jimmy smiled.

"Meet you at the house," Harmony said and then grinned. The Prospect had stopped, he thought he was safe with Jimmy through the gates, and the car was between them.

"Gotcha," Jimmy said and then leaned back and began to pull forward just as she shot the dirt at the Prospect's feet.

"SHIT!" the Prospect said and Fork bent over and laughed.

Jimmy slammed on the brakes, looked over his shoulder, and shook his head. "Fork, you need a lift?"

"Yeah, man, this is too much entertainment for me," Fork said and went to the car and got in. "Creed, you got our woman."

"Fuck yeah, Annie Oakley and me will be along soon," Creed said with a grin.

"You do not ever mess with my business," she yelled at the young man who was glaring at her. "EVER!"

"I think someone needs to get out of the compound for a minute or two." Creed laughed and Harmony dropped her arm to the side, looked at Creed, and smiled.

"Yay!" she cried.

"Come on, let's get your info and you can go with Jimmy to pick up the package at the post office," Creed said.

"Cool," she said and climbed on the back of his bike and flipped off the Prospect that was still glaring at her and closing the gate. "See you in a few, asshole."

"Damn, we are going to lose the guy if you keep this up," Creed muttered.

"Pussy," Harmony shrugged.

*****

"You know someone named Lola?" Jimmy said, Creed cussed, and Fork slammed his bottle of beer on the desk.

"Yep," Harmony said. "They fucked her and then kicked her out of the club when she went psycho."

"Oh good," Jimmy laughed. "You know what we are dealing with. She is in with the Diablos. Put a guy on her, I would bet that she leads us to the main guy because she has been strutting around the Savages' town like a bitch in heat."

"Fuck," Fork yelled.

"That's all I got so far, I will keep you updated," Jimmy said and then looked at Harmony while Creed said.

"Go into town with Jimmy, take a breather, when you get back we'll go over what we need done to lock down this place."

They were hiding something from her, she knew it. With a shrug she got up and walked out the door with her friend.

Chapter Eleven

"We got a lock on how they are getting in yet?" Creed barked to Easy and Poke who had come over right after Harmony left.

Easy nodded. "Found one entrance they had used, and we are looking for more. It was freshly dug in, haven't had time to send anyone down yet to see where it leads. We need to seal up the entrances first, then we will hunt."

Fork smiled. "Hunting is my favorite sport."

"Yeah well, looks like we are going to get plenty of practice. There were probably fifty footprints around the entrance we found," Poke said.

"Shit," Creed muttered.

"Yeah and we are going to need to talk to Shady about moving the weapons for the time being, one of the prints led right to the Shed, they know where we store the guns," Easy growled.

"Great, people coming onto our land, fucking Lola is on Savages' land, and Diablos all over the fucking place. What the fuck is going on?" Fork said.

"We need to have church, call the guys get them here now, I am not wasting anytime with this shit. Everyone is coming into the compound. Lockdown. I will call the Savages, let them know what they are coming into, make sure they know who they are bringing. We need to firm up the deal with them. They are trying to take us both out and if we don't pay attention, they could succeed," Creed said.

The guys agreed and they made plans. Harmony had been cooped up on the compound for three days and this wasn't going to make her happy. Because either her guys stayed here, or they were going to have to go through pat downs every time they came on the property.

*****

"Starbucks!!" Harmony yelled and Jimmy laughed.

"Okay, boss," he said and pulled into the parking lot of her favorite coffee place.

"Four days, I have not had Starbucks in four days," she whispered. "I am going to buy two, one for now one for when I am done, and an everything bagel with cream cheese, and a blueberry scone."

Jimmy laughed and shook his head, he opened the door, looked around. They had a Prospect following them, and he nodded to the guy. "He want something?" Jimmy asked over the hood of the car and she paused and looked back.

"Damn," she said. "I suppose, I shot at him too I think. Go get his order and come on in."

"Right, boss," he said and went to ask the young man what he wanted. With a shake of her head, Harmony turned and hopped into the coffee shop. She stopped and closed her eyes and breathed in the delicious scent. Damn, she missed this place.

She walked to the counter and waited. There was only one man ahead of her and she was bouncing with anticipation. She looked over her shoulder and saw Jimmy talking to the Prospect and laughing, he was going to have to order his own shit then, she wasn't waiting.

When it was her turn she ordered exactly what she wanted, the woman chirped happily in front of her something about having a nice day or some shit like that and Harmony moved on. Like she needed to be told to have a nice day, she was getting two Carmel Frappuccinos and food, she was in heaven.

Harmony grabbed the spork the woman gave her to spread her cream cheese and she frowned. "Sorry, out of knives."

Harmony shrugged and went to a table and sat down. She put the straw in the cup before she opened the stupid spork packet and Jimmy walked in.

"Gimme a minute," he called and she waved at him, yeah like it mattered, she had a delicate procedure to preform. Spreading the cream cheese was an art form, one she had perfected over the last few years. It was an addiction, and she wasn't giving it up.

She heard someone approach her but Harmony didn't look up, she needed to get the cream cheese before it cooled down or it wouldn't melt correctly.

"Hey, *puta*," a voice said to her.

Harmony smiled but didn't look up. "Hey," she replied.

"You finally crawled out of your hole? We been looking for you, wanting to see if you liked our gift?" the man sneered. This time she did look up. And a young Hispanic man stood in front of her table with three men in back of him all smiling and laughing. Harmony grinned and shook her head.

"What gift?" she asked and went back to her bagel, but not before she took a long drink of her orgasmic blended coffee drink.

"Your campfire, *puta*, we wanted to see if you liked your campfire and invite you to come with us, we have more surprises for you." The man laughed.

"Oh?" Harmony laughed and smiled when she finished the bottom piece and then started in on the top piece. "Another present? That is awful nice of you, but I am a little busy today, I have a billion things on my plate. Right after I am done here, I have an appointment for a pap smear, I have been itchy down there the last few weeks, and I am pretty sure I need some medication. Maybe you should find someone else for your '*little*' surprise."

The man kicked the table and Harmony frowned and then looked back up at him. She shook her head and then turned to see where Jimmy was, her friend was ordering and not paying attention. She was going to have to talk to him about that, if she were a normal woman who needed protection she would be fucked right now. Then she turned to see the Prospect who was staring at a car in the parking lot, which she assumed belonged to these assholes because it was a low rider.

"Fuck you, *puta*," the man growled. "You need to get off your fucking fat ass and come with us, we have orders."

Harmony smiled at him, then shrugged, and went back to putting the cream cheese on her bagel. "Well like I said, I am booked, because after the pap, I have another appointment. You see, I have to go and talk to a therapist about my anger issues; my biker boyfriends seem to think my fascination with blood is unusual. I don't, but they worry so much, it is cute."

"Stop fucking around with us," the man said, he was getting whispers from his friend behind him, which meant they were getting impatient, and not impressed with the way the leader was handling it. This could seriously be fun, because it sounded like they were egging him on. Idiots still thought she was alone.

"Not fucking around, especially with you, I told you 'LITTLE' is not my style, I like more than what you got, from the looks of you. Shit, from that little bulge, you are nowhere near what I am used to. My men are fucking huge, shit, when they fucked me I could barely get out of bed, felt that shit for like days." She smiled happily and then paused, her spork worked, she was happy about that.

The leader finally lost his patience and kicked her table harder, this time her bagel went flying onto the floor and her drink tipped to the side. Harmony managed to grab her drinks for a second before the guy grabbed her neck, pulled her out of her seat, and held her firmly in front of him.

She heard Jimmy yell, and then saw the Prospect out of the corner of her eye run toward the door. There were too many people, the whole place had exploded when her drinks hit the floor and they saw the men grab her. Jimmy was pushing his way through but he just wasn't close enough.

"*Puta*, enough shit, let's go," he said and shook her a little. She figured most women would cry and whimper but she was just pissed off. He fucking ruined her goddamn Frappuccinos and bagel, and the greaser kept calling her bitch, that was so not okay.

"Hey," she yelled into his face, even though his hand squeezed her throat, she didn't stop. "Fucktard, what is wrong with you. That was my bagel you knocked on the floor. There is no excuse for being a bagel killer."

His friends made noises of irritation; they wanted her under control, well that was so not going to happen. But she heard them speaking in rapid Spanish to each other, and from the sounds of their voices, it wasn't looking like they were going to walk away.

The leader shook her again and then took a step and ignored his friends, she had gotten under his skin. He pulled her down until she was bent over, standing over her bagel, which was on the floor in front of her, and he lifted his foot and stepped on her bagel. Harmony saw red, and then she did what she had to do, no one fucked with her Starbucks.

The guy was laughing, and he was lifting her up, pulling her toward the back door by her neck and Jimmy was yelling. He had made it to the middle of the mayhem and two of the man's friends were blocking him and began swinging. The Prospect was on the phone yelling at someone but he was still too far away, none of the customers were lifting a finger and when she turned she saw why, the last idiot was holding a gun in front of him and staring at the crowd, as if daring them to move to help her. Harmony had enough, they had ruined her morning and she was sure at this point it was Creed and Fork on the other end of the phone. They were going to be pissed at her and never let her out of the compound again.

She planted her foot, and gripped the spork, which she still miraculously had in her hand and swung her arm up in an arch with all the power she could muster. Thankfully, she caught him at a good angle and the spork sunk right into his neck muscle right where it joined his shoulder. He screamed and released her. Harmony didn't pause, she kicked quickly at the guy holding the gun and sent it flying through the air since he didn't have a good grip on it. That one took off running. Jimmy had one of the others on the ground while the Prospect was holding the other one by the neck just like the leader had done to her, the difference was, the Prospect was tall, and he had muscles, he had no problems putting the guy down as he tried to run by him.

"What the fuck, you bitch," the leader yelled.

"Bitch, you are calling me a bitch, you ruined my Starbucks experience, you fuckin' asshole," Harmony yelled down at him.

"Should we call the police?" the chirpy little Starbucks worker said.

Harmony rolled her eyes. "Yeah and an ambulance, the fucktard needs looked at." Blood was seeping between his fingers quite quickly Harmony noticed. "Better call the ambulance first, he is loosing blood fast."

"Yeah, Prez, she is fine," the Prospect was saying behind her.

"Fine?" Harmony yelled, "I am not fine, the bastards ruined my…"

"Starbuck experience, I know," the Prospect said dryly then frowned into the phone. "Hell no I am not bringing the leader in, he has a spork sticking out of his neck, they aren't gonna let me take him."

Harmony frowned and looked back at the leader laying on the ground moaning and acting like a little bitch. "Please, they are going to give him a few stitches. It's not like I stabbed him with a knife or something, they were out of knives or I would have, then he would have been worse off. Shit, he may die of fucking embarrassment, not being stabbed by a damn spork."

"Yeah, Prez, I got you," the Prospect said and shook his head and hung up the phone. "You are supposed to shut your mouth and sit your ass down and wait, they are on their way."

"Whatever," Harmony said and then smiled. "Hey, Starbucks chick, make me some new food, I have to wait here for my men."

*****

"What the fuck is wrong with you. You weren't like this two years ago, I would have fucking noticed. It's like you are someone else," Creed yelled as he stood over Harmony who was smiling and eating her new bagel. The police were there and they were taking statements. It was organized chaos until Creed and Fork showed up yelling.

"Honey," Harmony said and looked up. "Face it, you had no clue what you were getting into. You saw what you wanted to see, let me clue you in, you were wearing blinders. I have not nor have I ever been a sweet little girl who sat and took orders. My father never raised me like that. This is who I am, you fucked me after I shot at you so if you were honest, I am pretty sure you like the me you are staring at right now. If you don't, there is the fucking door, I am not going to change."

Fork stared down at her with a shocked expression on his face. "Are you kidding me right now. You are trying to give us our walking papers when you stabbed someone with a fucking spork? Babe, this is wacked."

"No, damn it," Harmony yelled and stood and pointed her finger at the guys. "What is fucking wacked is the fact you are standing here yelling at me for stabbing some guy with a spork after he tried to fucking kidnap me, in a Starbucks with one of your men and one of my men standing right fucking there. What is even more wacked is the fact I had to protect myself. Since I have walked back into your fucking compound I have shown you who I was, people have been telling you who I was, and everyone around you have clued into who I am. You two, on the other hand, still are fixated on the little shy chick you think I am."

Creed took a deep breath and then said with a roar, "We know who the fuck we have, Harmony. We actually did speak to people and we realized we were wrong. And we know who you are and we fucking like it, because, woman, we don't want a fucking shrinking violet, it would never work with us. But fuckin' A, woman, being a woman who can take care of herself and being a woman who shoots at my Prospects and stabs people in the fucking neck with a spork are two vastly different things. However, in no fucking way, shape, or form are either of us walking away from you goddamn it. Get it through your fucking head, babe, we are in it for the long haul, we said you were our old lady and we fucking meant it—meant it two years ago, mean it now. We can take anything you dish out because, babe, I know how to deal with your sass, but what I will not fucking take, is goddamn phone calls telling me you stabbed some guy who was fucking trying to kidnap you in the neck with a spork. You should have been the one to fucking call me and tell me about this shit, the second that prick approached you. We need to have a serious conversation about the way you are dealing with situations, babe."

Harmony shrugged and looked at her men, her heart melted a little more when she heard they weren't going to leave her. Seriously, she had been worried about that because not too many guys could handle her temper. But they did, and she was feeling warm and fuzzy about that. She would let them know later that she wasn't going to be yelled at in public. Now she was just happy to finish her bagel and frozen drink and let them deal with the fallout. She was exhausted from her outing.

"SPORK!" Shady yelled from the doorway and Harmony turned and grinned when she saw all of the bitches and half of the club coming in the door.

"What?" Harmony yelled.

"Your fucking name, bitch. It is Spork." Bob laughed and Harmony groaned and put her hand in her face.

Chapter Twelve

The party was in full swing, if you could call it that. *It had been a hell of a day*, Creed thought, *the last two days had been hell.* Shit, after the whole Starbucks incident, which is what the whole fucking club was referring to it as, things had been unsettled.

Their relationship with Harmony had been strained unless they were in bed fucking her brains out and making her come and admit she belonged to them. Other than that, their woman was driving them nuts. She continually came up with plans and solutions that put herself in harm's way and they were refusing to okay her fucked up plans. This led to more fights, which led to crazy fucking hot sex.

It started when Harmony and Jimmy had dug in and searched for Lola. They found out where she had been over the last two years and none of it looked fuckin' promising. She was wacked, and situations she was involved in tended to get wacked. They were all pissed they had missed this piece of the puzzle. Should have killed the bitch when he had the chance. Harmony wanted to rectify this oversight, she was ready to go into Savages' territory and just shoot the bitch down. Not happening until they knew how far the woman was into the Diablos, which was pretty far if the reports they were getting were any indication.

They were after the mine, the money, and the territory. Creed and Fork had called church and updated everyone in the club. It hadn't been a pleasant meeting, but the only good thing was that everyone was on the compound grounds and under watch. Tonight they were going to solidify their alliance and then make plans to take out the Diablos for good.

"The girls have a meet tomorrow at Bitches," Easy said as they were walking over to the main clubhouse.

"Yeah," Creed said. "We are going to have a meeting after tonight to discuss what goes on with the Savages."

"What about Harmony?" Fork laughed. "She has been itching to go to Bitches."

"We can take her, she can hang with Shady and the girls while we meet." Creed laughed.

"Learn some moves?" Poke joked.

"Tell Free to teach her the pole dance." Fork clapped his hand on Easy's shoulder. "We can install one in the upstairs."

As they walked in Creed took in the scene, Tonto and the other Savages were settled into the sectionals on one side of the clubhouse, and the Warriors across the room, it was like there was an invisible line dividing the two groups. They had to get the two groups talking but the tension was thick. In the middle was the bar and Raven and Kink were manning it silently. The only movement in the room was men getting up to get their beers. The music played in the background and it still didn't help the silence.

"Gotta make this cool," Fork said and looked over to the Savages.

"Yeah, feels like a fucking ice cream social." Easy laughed.

"Where are the girls?" Creed asked, looking around. They hadn't come in yet, Harmony and the other women were giving them a chance to get used to being in the same room with each other and measuring dicks. Before the party, they had warned her to be cool, and she had agreed, for once.

"Taking shots upstairs." Poke laughed. "Free is already drunk."

"Hell yeah," Easy laughed and rubbed his hands together.

"A drunk Free is a horny Free," Poke said and held up his fist for Easy to bump.

"Oh shit," Fork laughed and they all turned. Here came the ladies and yes, they were drunk, and loud, and dressed to fucking kill.

Shady led the way with a black leather vest, with apparently nothing on under it, she wore her leather pants and biker boots, and her hair was a mess around her shoulders. All of the women were wearing black leather in various styles but it was Harmony who drew his attention, shit, she was wearing short leather shorts and a black halter top. Her tits looked like they were about ready to bust out of the top. She wore thigh high leather boots that he imagined wrapped around his waist.

She walked directly to him and Fork; with a grin, she sat down on his lap and wrapped her arms around his neck. "Hey, sweetie," she whispered into his ear and he smiled. *Fuck, she was theirs.*

"Babe," Fork said and turned her head by grabbing her hair that was secured in a leather wrap and tugging. She smiled, turned, and then kissed him soundly.

"What's up?" Shady said, motioning to the other side of the room with her head.

"Not much, talked to them when they came in, didn't bring any of their women, didn't want to start shit. Just waiting to see if we are going to be able to make this shit work," Creed said. "A lot of bad blood."

Harmony frowned and then shook her head. "Needs to be buried."

"Let's get a shovel," Bob said and grinned then walked to the bar and slapped her hand down. The women laughed and waited. "Shots all around," Bob called out and the guys all raised their eyebrows in surprise.

"Shit," Fork said, stood and went to the bar. He whispered into Bob's ear and the woman rolled her eyes and then walked back to where they were sitting. Fork remained at the bar and waited, not looking at Tonto or the other Savages. It only took a moment for his brother to rise and walk to the bar and stand next to Fork, he raised his chin and waited.

Harmony grinned when Raven put a shot down for both of them and they turned to each other and nodded. They drank their shots and slammed the glass back down on the bar and then did the man chest bump and the tension left the room. Harmony stood and let out a howl and the party was on!

Fork walked back to Creed and lifted his chin and Harmony threw her arms around him and kissed him.

The evening progressed and the Savages and Warriors finally started to intermix—thankfully. It seemed their call for peace was working for now.

Creed and Fork were talking to Tonto and Sandman when he heard Harmony say something to one of the Savages.

"Do your women have tats? Do any of them ride themselves, Shady does here, I am pretty sure she could take some of your guys," she stated.

He didn't hear the reply but then he heard her go on, shit. "Oh well we do, we are all gonna get the same tats because we are the Warrior Bitches."

Creed grimaced; he hadn't had a chance to tell the club about the girls' plan, too much shit had happened they needed to deal with. Sharing with the Savages their plans with the girls had not been the cards.

"Who are you?" the man asked with humor.

"Harmony," their woman replied. "Creed and Fork's woman." Creed smiled when he heard her refer to herself as theirs, Fork was sitting to the side, and he heard it too and smiled. Yep, it was sinking in, finally.

"You don't have a tat already?" The man laughed. "Then you are not their woman."

Creed froze, *shit, fucking asshole*. He heard Harmony suck in a breath and then she said, "Yes, I am."

"Sweetheart, if you were my woman, I would have marked your ass before you even stepped foot outside my bedroom." The biker laughed.

"CREED! FORK!" Harmony bellowed and both men grimaced, *stupid fucker*, Creed thought when he leaned back and yelled.

"Yeah, babe."

"Why don't I have a tattoo?" she yelled and glared at him.

"'Cause it is your body and I don't tell my woman what to do with her body," Creed yelled back and Fork yelled an agreement. Harmony grinned and nodded, then turned back to the guys and winked.

"See, I am theirs."

"I am just saying, most bikers want to see their marks on their women." He shrugged and then Harmony frowned and bit her lip. Shady was next to her laughing and she leaned over and listened while Harmony was whispering furiously. Creed caught Fork's eye, shrugged, and went back to his conversation. They were solidifying their plans with Tonto and Sandman finally.

Creed lost sight of Harmony but the music got louder and the drinks flowed more. When the Savages' leaders stood to leave they shook hands. The stoic Tonto looked at him and nodded then said, "You may want to get your woman. We are out."

Creed frowned and then turned, they had been talking for a few hours and he saw all the women in a circle at the end of a bar, a table was in the center and he could see the legs of Harmony on the table but that was it.

Fork rolled his eyes as they saw the Savages out of the house. A loud whistle from their leader and they were gone.

"Went well," Fork said.

"Yeah, think this is gonna be good for us. They said next time we would have the whole club. First we need to get our security down completely," Creed said and they began to walk to where Harmony was laying.

"No one got down and dirty, which is good." Fork laughed. They had all agreed while the Savages were here no one was going to fuck, it was strictly a drinking only party until they left. Then they could cut loose. They didn't wait apparently. Because he could see Maxi already grabbing Candy's tit and pulling her to the sectionals. The tension had eased.

"So fucking cool. I am next," Bob yelled, as they got closer to the table. Creed pushed past the women and frowned.

Harmony was on her stomach on the table, Kink was leaning over her with his tat gun and was putting an intricate tat on her shoulder. Fork laughed as he leaned over, it was the one Shady had shown him a few days ago that they had designed for the Warrior Bitches. The Ops Warriors and the one they designed were combined. Kink was just finishing the word underneath.

"What does it say?" Creed asked Fork who was closer.

"Creed, Spork, Fork" his friend laughed and Creed rolled his eyes. Only his woman would write Spork on her shoulder.

*****

Later that night, Creed traced his finger over Harmony's new tat, it was hot, and Fork and he had both shown their appreciation for her new ink.

"You like that?" Harmony muttered on her stomach.

"Yeah, babe, I like that," Creed whispered and leaned over and kissed her shoulder.

"What do you like about it?" Harmony asked.

Fork laughed. "Babe, a chick tats our names on her skin, that is fucking hot. Especially when she is our woman, the one we have been waiting for."

Harmony rolled over, looked at them, and frowned. "You don't think I was just being weird, I mean we could break up, you could dump me, then I am stuck with these weird ass tats on me."

"When are you going to get it?" Creed said, staring down at her seriously.

"Get what?" Harmony frowned.

Creed sighed and Fork turned her face to him. "We are not going to dump you, we are not going to change our minds. We decided two years ago you were ours. I can't explain it, we just fit. The time we are together, learning new things about you, I can tell you, that everything you show us makes me love you more than what I do when I wake up in the morning."

"You love me?" she whispered and her heart stopped.

Creed laughed. "When you walked into the compound and began yelling at us, I knew we had missed out. When you unlocked yourself from the handcuffs, I knew we had found our match. But, babe, that first time you came apart in our arms and fucking screamed our names. You owned us.

You own us, we own you. If it makes you feel better, I will tat your name wherever you want on me because there is nothing in this world that will take you away from us."

Harmony felt the tears gathering in her eyes. "You love me?"

"Yeah, babe, we love you," Fork said and kissed her gently and then laughed when Harmony pulled back and began to yell.

"Holy shit, you love me!" She cried and hugged them both.

"Get your ass down here, babe." Fork laughed as she jumped on the bed between them.

"Fine," Harmony laughed and then laid back down between them.

Fork reached up, trailed his finger down her neck to her breast, and circled her nipple. It stood at attention as he teased her. Creed leaned in and licked her other straining nipple and she had to fight the urge to grab the back of their heads and put them where she wanted them. The moisture was flowing between her legs and she rubbed her thighs together. Shit, this was so much more, knowing they loved her and would do anything to protect her. Fuck, this was all consuming, and she wanted to wrap them in her love and show them she could be the woman they needed.

Creed let his hand drift down her stomach and then to her pussy. He pushed two fingers into her forcefully and she moaned. *Fuck yeah*, she thought and moved her hips as he ground his hand in her wet cunt. Fork kissed her passionately and wasn't giving her a chance to catch her breath, she was on to them, they loved doing this to her. If they kept her breathless and on edge, she would come so many times they had been keeping count now. There was something about them both touching her and the feel of their four hands on her that drove her to distraction.

Fork pulled back and looked down at her, then he began to kiss his way down one side of her neck while Creed joined him and started on the other side, finally, both of them latched on to her nipples at the same time and she threw her head back and moaned. The dual sensations were enough to drive her wild, but add to the difference of the mouths, and she was wiggling with pent up need. Damn it, this is what they did every single time to her.

"I'm gonna have my nighttime snack," Creed murmured against her now peaked nipple and kissed his way down her stomach. She felt his hot breath on her mound and wanted to beg him to hurry.

Fork palmed the breast Creed just left and continued to suck and nip at her, making her writhe under him. "I love your breasts; they are perfect, just like you. Babe, I need you to touch me," he whispered. She moved her arm between them, trailed her hand down his taunt stomach, and finally grasped his thick hard cock. It was weepy with pre-cum already. She smoothed the thick liquid around the tip of his head and then tugged him up. She almost screamed when Creed swiped her pussy lips. She had been so focused on the job at hand, that she forgot where Creed was.

Creed had settled her thighs over his shoulders and used his fingers to hold her open for him. Spearing her with his tongue and then licking up to her clit in a fast and relentless rhythm that was driving her mad. Harmony clutched Fork's cock a little firmer and began to stroke him in the same rhythm that Creed set.

Creed looked up and said, "Sweetest thing I have ever tasted."

She rolled her eyes and then groaned when she felt Creed begin to use her own juices and rub his thumb on her back entrance. She loved their dirty talk.

Fork pulled out of her hand and said, "Not coming in your hand, babe, gonna come in your mouth, want you swallowing me down and loving every drop of it. Later I will fuck your cunt and empty into you, Creed will take you mouth and you will be full to the top with us."

She grinned and nodded, "Do your best," as Fork moved to lay on the pillows, his hard, straining cock tantalizing her by bobbing right in front of her face. She couldn't resist leaning forward and giving it a quick swipe with her tongue to get the taste of him. Fork groaned and then moved quicker while Creed helped position her on her hands and knees.

Once they were in place, she grinned and looked up at Fork, who was looking like he was in a little pain. "This is my favorite position, 'cause I can feel you both come at the same time and watch."

"Thor would love for you to get to know him better," Fork said jokingly and then grabbed his cock by the base and waved it at her.

"What the fuck?" Creed said, lifting his head from where he had still been licking her pussy from behind.

"Thor?" She giggled and rested her head on his thigh while trying to catch her breath.

"What? Don't tell me you haven't named your cock, asshole. I know for a fact the chick in Cali called your cock 'Thundershock'," Fork grumbled.

"Talk about a deflator, man, what the hell is wrong with you?" Creed said.

"Hey, if you have a problem with my naming my cock, then it's your problem. Thor is still ready for action." Fork laughed.

By this time, Harmony was threatening to fall over to her side because she was laughing so hard, but Creed held her in place. She had never had fun during sex, this was a first, and she kinda liked it. Creed slapped her ass playfully and said, "Get back to work; apparently Thor needs a little love, while Thundershock here is getting ready to shake your world."

She nodded and giggled a little more, but then the laugh quickly turned into a moan as she felt Fork tweak both of her nipples as she rose and Creed used two fingers to spear her pussy hard and fast. She was so wet. His fingers just slid in with no resistance and she began to feel her wetness gather again.

"Yeah, sweetheart, cream for me," Creed said and continued to pump his fingers in and out of her while she tried to concentrate on Fork, who was holding his cock in front of her lips. Fuck, he was gorgeous.

Licking around the head, making sure she cleaned the head. She pulled the tip of his cock into her mouth and swirled her tongue around the top. Fork groaned and then she took him in a little further and teased the backside of his head, just under the top fold—it was a sensitive area for a man; she discovered it a few years ago with a demanding boyfriend.
"Fuckin' A, honey, where the hell did you learn that?" Fork yelled when she swept her tongue over the sensitive area again and sucked hard.
Creed chuckled and said, "Give me a minute, and she won't be teasing anymore."
Creed pulled his fingers out of her and then lined up his cock with her pussy. "You ready, baby? You're gonna be stuffed with our cocks," Creed said, grasped her hips, causing her to groan around Fork's cock.
Fork wrapped a hand in her hair and she lowered her mouth slowly down his shaft until it hit the back of her throat. Shit, she was only halfway down. Harmony grasped the base of his cock with one hand and began working her hand in time with her mouth.
Creed pushed slowly inside her tight pussy and he panted. "Holy shit, you are so tight. Man, she fits me like a glove."
She wanted to smile as they talked about her. They had no idea what those words did to her. Harmony had been waiting for two years—for this—and knowing they loved her made this all the more awesome. She and the guys had slipped into each other's lives like they had always belonged there, just like it should be. She was reveling in the feeling of closeness around them, knowing they cared for her. This was the final step of joining with them in her eyes. She was marked and claimed by them, there was nothing left in her eyes—she would be theirs forever. That was how she was made up.
When Creed was finally seated in her to the hilt, she took a deep breath around Fork's cock and then swallowed. Fork moaned again and the hand in her hair tightened. Creed pulled back and she was naturally pulled back with

him, allowing Fork's cock to slide out to the tip. Then Creed pushed back quickly and Fork's cock slid down her throat again, stopping where her hand had been stroking.

Harmony closed her eyes and turned her body over to them. Creed directed the symphony of movements while Fork encouraged both of them and talked about what he was seeing and feeling.

"That is so sexy, watching Creed pumping in and out of you. I can see your juices running down your thighs, I can't wait to get a taste of that, baby. Oh, man, and your mouth. Every time you hit that spot, I feel like I'm going to shoot my load right then."

Moving faster, Fork had to stop talking because the feelings were becoming intense. They could all feel the passion building, getting ready to flow over them. It was a glorious feeling to be between these two men. She thought about what they had talked about before and her pussy began to quiver at the thought of both of them fucking her at the same time. Creed shifted a little, and with each of his strokes, he hit her clit and she knew it wasn't going to be long before she exploded. Fork cried out that he was getting ready.

Creed reached around her easily, held her up, and then said loudly, "Come." And all three of them released the tension and felt their release flow through them. Harmony swallowed every last drop before collapsing in a quivering mess on top of Fork with Creed sandwiching her, lying on her back.

"I can't move," Harmony said and then felt Creed roll over to the side, taking her with him so she was laying half on top of both of the men. The sweat was causing her to chill as it finally cooled down and Creed threw a cover over them.

"Nap time, we have an hour before we have to get cleaned up again."

"Ohhh sounds nice," she said sleepily, then snuggled between them, and quickly fell asleep.

Tonight was about love, but reality was going to hit them tomorrow and it was going to hurt, the only thing Harmony did know, was that she was never going to let them go.

Chapter Thirteen

Shady and the girls had a meeting to go over schedules and routines. Harmony had been begging to go to one of their meetings because she wanted to see the inside of Bitches, and she also wanted the girls to teach her some moves they had. It was something she had never thought about, her dancing, but after hearing about Free's impromptu dance at the clubhouse, she was interested in learning something for her men.

"See ya," Harmony said against Creed's lips. They were all going to the club but Shady and the girls were riding in cars. This decision was made after learning the Diablos were given the order to shoot the women off the back of the bikes. No one was taking the chance one of the women would get hurt. They knew this had to come from that bitch, Lola, but they still hadn't gotten a bead on her and until they knew who she was hiding with, they were on hold.

"Watch your back, babe," Creed said and pulled her closer. She sighed and accepted his kiss. She loved them.

"I will," she murmured and then grinned when she felt Fork slap her ass and turn her around.

"Ordered our own pole, woman. Go learn me a new routine," Fork demanded and Harmony giggled and nodded.

"Gotcha, I have to make sure Thor and Thundershock are happy."

"You know it," Fork said and kissed her and then turned.

"Let's ride," he said to Creed who rolled his eyes but followed his friend. Harmony watched them walk away in their worn jeans that hugged their asses. Shit, she was getting herself worked up.

Shady stepped to her side and laughed. "Come on, Spork, we got some work to do."

"Can one of those things we have to work on be finding me a new name, Spork is just creepy," Harmony complained.

"You tatted it on your shoulder, I am pretty sure that is on you now," Bob yelled from the back seat and Harmony laughed.

Freedom, Nike, Rain, and Treat were in the other car and surrounding them were six bikers. *They looked like they were having a fuckin' parade*, Harmony thought, *but whatever made the guys happy*. They had been serious about keeping them safe.

The only good part was the bikers would follow them to the club and then they would be in their own meeting. They wouldn't be following them every moment of the day.

Shady blasted the music and Harmony laughed as they sang to the songs. It only took five minutes to get to Bitches and as they pulled into the parking lot, she smiled when she saw all the bikes. They were all here already.

The girls got out of the cars and all began to file into the club, they were laughing and joking.

"Shit," Shady said and Harmony paused.

"What?" she asked as the girls went in the entrance.

"Forgot my bag," Shady said. "Be right back."

"I will come with you. Go ahead, guys, we are on property, will be there in a sec," Harmony said and turned to walk back to the car with Shady.

As one moment in time, changed everything.

*****

"Do you know what really pisses me off?" the drug lord asked Shady and Harmony as they walked back to Bitches from the car.

Both women froze but then Shady turned and answered coldly. "Fuck you."

"Women who don't know their place," the man said and laughed. "What makes you think you could ever have beaten me."

"Well, Dom," Shady sneered and Harmony jumped because her friend obviously knew the man standing behind them pointing a gun at them. Shit, her gun was in her bag, she couldn't go for it without wasting time. "You would know everything about women right, because you have held onto yours right?"

Dom grinned and Harmony shivered. He was scary, and not scary hot biker dude, he was scary freaking psycho dude. Dom whoever he was had black hair that looked exactly like Shady's, and eyes that were the same ice blue color, the difference was Shady had life in hers, this guy's were dead. He was tall and thin, and if she met him on the street wearing his black silk suit, she would have thought he was a businessman. Seeing him with a gun in his hand, Harmony figured they just met the guy who was behind all of the shit.

"Francesca, you never should have run away." Dom laughed.

Harmony frowned and then looked at her friend. "Wait, Francesca? Your name is Francesca?"

Shady laughed and smiled at Harmony. "Yeah, I kinda changed that right away, you know how embarrassing it is to have the nickname Franny? It sucked when I was young."

"Well yeah," Harmony agreed. "I mean, torture, Franny, ugh I can't even say it without thinking of an old lady with ugly underwear."

"I know right." Shady laughed.

She knew what Harmony was doing. Harmony had slowly moved so she was turned to Shady's side, her purse was hidden then, and she was moving her hand slowly to find her gun.

"Shut up," Dom growled. "I am thinking you are not appreciating your position."

This time it was Harmony's turn to answer. "Because we aren't, nothing you can do will stop the shit storm coming your way, asshole. Coming onto Warriors' property has signed your death warrant."

Dominic Reyes smiled and shook his head. "Little girl, I am safe as I would be if I were at my own house. Too bad you will not be around to actually see your friends die, oh, and when you see him in hell, let him know I am sorry I missed out on the family reunion."

He laughed and looked over his shoulder and Harmony followed his gaze. The backdoor had been chained even though she could see someone or something was pushing to get out. The front door was probably the same way. Shit, well now she was going to have to think on her feet.

"Franny," Harmony said quietly.

"Yeah, Spork," Shady said just as quietly.

"Who is this?" Harmony asked.

"My brother, Dominic Reyes III," she said and then spit on the ground. "Fucking bastard who ruined my life."

"Shit," Harmony responded and then pulled the gun from her purse and turned to fire.

Dom though had already been prepared. Both of the women felt the burn of the bullet entering their bodies. *Shit*, Harmony thought, reaching for her friend, *the guys were going to be seriously pissed off*.

*****

"The Savages are going to start looking for Lola and where they are holed up at," Creed said to the club. The meeting had just started and they were getting to business right away.

"Harmony has her men looking into several of the Diablos who are running their mouths," Fork added. "One thing we do know, is this is not only about drugs. This is personal, and they are looking not only to set up shop here, they want to take over. They want the mine. We know they have been on the compound, and the shit has been locked down. We need to see where the tunnels lead us."

"For now we are going to play this close to the vest. No one leaves the compound without backup. The women and children are on the compound until further notice, the only ones allowed to leave are the Bitches, and they will be guarded every second. We need to have the girls rally and get things set, supplies brought in, 'cause more men are coming. Called Cali and Montana, they had shit to deal with up until now, but they are coming," Creed said and they heard one of the Prospects yell from the hallway.

"What did he say?" Fork said and stood.

"Someone chained the doors," Easy said and stood.

The room emptied as the men went to the entrances. Creed and Fork stepped into the main room of the strip club where the women were already standing looking confused.

Creed searched the floor and couldn't find Harmony, shit, or Shady.

"Where is Harmony?" Creed barked out and the Prospect stepped up.

"Shady and her went to go get Shady's bag in the car," the Prospect said.

"By themselves?" Fork yelled and the Prospect winced.

"They were on our property," the Prospect said weakly.

"Guarded means fucking guarded," Creed yelled and went to the backdoor and pushed. It didn't move.

"Fucking windows are shatterproof," Fork said as a chair bounced off the window.

"Can you see them?" Creed asked.

"No," Fork said. "The corner of the building is blocking me."

"Upstairs," Poke yelled and they ran for the top floor, the windows overlooked the parking lot in the back.

Easy was ordering everyone to help try to bust the doors down and they could hear the pounding already. Creed and Fork ran up the stairs and as they looked out the back window, both of them grew cold. A man was holding a gun on Shady and Harmony.

"Get me outside," Creed yelled loudly.

"Shit, Creed," Fork whispered as they watched the scene unfold in front of them.

They heard a crash and knew Easy had somehow found a way out of the building but they were frozen. The man raised his gun as Harmony turned with one in her hand and shot. Right before their eyes, Shady and Harmony fell to the ground.

As the man turned, Creed looked at his cold eyes. He stared up for a brief moment at Creed and Fork and then smiled and walked away. Fork grabbed him by the arm and they ran; the only thing they could think of was getting to their woman, praying when they reached her she was still alive. There was no other option.

*****

"Harmony?" she heard someone call. "Harmony, come on and wake up."

It was Creed, she could tell by the pissed off tone of his voice and she frowned. *Why the fuck was he pissed* as she tried to open her eyes, but they wouldn't open though. *Shit, what the fuck?* she thought, and tried harder, then she remembered. *Shady's fucking psycho brother shot me. Where did he shoot me?*

"Harmony, I am gonna fucking spank that ass until you can't sit down for a week if you don't fucking open your eyes," Creed barked.

"I don't think this is what the nurse meant by talk to her." Fork laughed.

"Only thing she responds to, stubborn bitch," Creed said.

Harmony lay and listened as she took inventory of her body, she felt something on her arm, a bandage. *Well at least they hadn't gotten her in the head,* she thought, *would have seriously sucked.* Her head was fuzzy; she couldn't seem to make herself do what she wanted, like open her eyes.

"I am not fucking around, Harmony," Creed said.

"Damn," she murmured. "I am pretty sure you are supposed to bring flowers when someone is shot, not fucking call them a bitch."

"Thank God," Fork said and leaned over. "Babe, open your eyes."

"They don't want to," she murmured.

"Do it anyway," Creed ordered and she frowned. Concentrating, she focused and finally felt her eyelids moving. *Shit, the light, that fucking hurt.*

"Shady?" she whispered.

"She's in surgery," Fork said back.

"Where?" she asked.

"Right here, babe," Creed said.

"No, where did she get shot?" Harmony asked.

"In the chest, babe," Creed said.

"Fuck," Harmony cried and then opened her eyes fully. She felt the tears already forming, she had let her friend down damn it, if she had only been quicker. What the fuck was she going to do without Shady, she was the only one who understood her. She was her sister, her best friend, her head Bitch. Damn it.

"Hang on, babe, let me call the nurse. They gave you some shit. You have stitches, bullet entered and exited in the fatty part of your upper arm. They cleaned it, got the bleeding stopped and stitched you up. But they had to sedate you because you wouldn't let go of Shady. Fuck, I have never heard anything like it. You screamed her name and held on so tight, babe. Broke my heart," Creed whispered.

"Scared the shit out of me, I didn't know where the blood was coming from. Easy and Poke had to knock out the front window so we could get out, bastards had the club rigged. They were going to blow us up after they left. You two saved us by going back to the car. If they wouldn't have had to waste time actually trying to kill you two, we would all be dead," Fork said and Harmony frowned.

"I gotta get up, she needs me," Harmony said.

"Wait for the nurse, if she says you are good, we will go to the waiting room, everyone else is already there. We have called the Savages, they are backing us up right now outside, guarding. Called the chapters already, we have men coming in to help. This is going to turn into a blood bath, babe, but seriously, they signed their death sentence when they fucking shot you and Shay," Creed said.

"It was her brother," Harmony said.

"What?" Fork said, looking confused.

"The man behind all this, Dom Reyes III. Shay told me right before he shot us. He is her brother, and he is the reason why she ran, I know it. She hates him. Her eyes, I have never seen that much hate in them," Harmony whispered.

"What the hell does he have to do with any of this?" Creed asked.

"He said she ran away," Harmony said.

"She did," Fork said absently. "Ran away from home I mean, she told us once, said she was running from an abusive family. I assumed it was her father and mother."

"I don't think so," Harmony said. "And I don't think it was the hitting kind of abuse either, he was fucking creepy. The way he looked at her."

"Remember that night she was in the mine offices?" Creed said.

They nodded, who could forget that night; she had been beaten so bad Harmony hadn't even recognized her when she saw her when she came to help her. That was the turning point of their relationship, that was when they had become sisters. Because that night, Harmony knew what happened to Shay and no one else did, only her because she had promised not to tell.

"Yeah," Harmony shivered.

"She kept saying that night he found her, somehow he found her and he was never going to let her go," Creed said grimly.

"I thought she said she didn't know her attacker," Fork said slowly.

"She did afterward. I also believe her, I don't think she realized what she was saying that night. I think it triggered something," Creed said and Harmony closed her eyes.

"Shit," she whispered.

"Yeah, shit is right," Creed said.

"We need to know everything we can about Dominic Reyes III and fast. I will make some calls, get people on this now," Fork said, pulling out his phone.

"Get me out of here, and I will find everything there is to know about this bastard," Harmony growled.

"Babe, you are on the sidelines until you heal," Creed said and Harmony snapped her head toward him.

"No, Creed, I am not," she snapped and then pushed the blanket back and snapped again. "Get the nurse and get the fuck out of my way. I need to go make sure my girl is going to live, because if she doesn't, I will burn this fucking town to the ground finding my revenge."

"We are with you, babe," Fork said gently.

Harmony paused, took a deep breath, and then looked at her men. She felt the tears threatening again and this time she couldn't hold them in. She hated crying, made her nose snot but damn it, this way Shady.

"She was so frightened that night when we came to clean her up. So frightened. I will never forget how broken she seemed. It was like someone had reached inside her and blew out her light. The whole time we were cleaning her she kept mumbling about it."

Creed frowned. "She didn't remember."

"Not that night, she didn't know who that was either, but they only beat her. No, she talked about HIM, I didn't know it was her brother, she only said HIM. The shit he did, my God, I don't know how she survived. I would never have been able to. She has scars, hidden in her tats, scars from what he did to her. All of it came back, because whoever beat her said he was coming for her. That is what HE used to tell her. That she could never run because HE would always come for her. It took me hours to get her to calm down and not to run. She was ready to pack up and leave. Said she was never going to be safe. Damn it, I told her HE would never find her here. The club was her new family, that you would take care of her. I promised," Harmony cried and Fork and Creed surrounded her, took her pain, and planted it on their shoulders.

"That night," Fork said with a frown. "After we kicked out Lola, remember what she said. She said she knew who could make us pay."

"Lola said a lot of shit," Creed growled.

"What if she had been working with him for longer than we thought?" Fork said.

"Lola was here for two years, been gone for another two," Creed reminded him. "That is a long time to work through a plan."

"Yeah, but she fucked up several times. We need to go back and look at shit. Because I swear I am right," Fork said and Creed nodded. "Add that to the list."

"Dom," Harmony whispered. "He is behind all of this, I know it. The first thing he said was he was pissed off that a woman would think she could beat him."

"Beat him at what though?" Fork asked.

"I don't know, but Shady needs to make it through, because I have a promise to keep to her," Creed said with a hard tone. "No one is going to hurt her on my watch again. I am done dicking around with this asshole. He is going to pay in more ways than one for this shit."

"I agree," Fork said. "I am also going to make a suggestion."

Creed closed his eyes, shit, he knew this was coming. She was going to go off the fucking deep end at them.

"Yeah," Creed agreed. "I will make the call."

"Who are you calling?" Harmony asked and looked at the two men who were looking like they were in pain.

"The one man who is going to be able to get through to Shady," Creed said.

Harmony looked confused. As far as she knew, Shady had never had a steady boyfriend. She had always said there wasn't anyone who could handle her for long, and vice versa as well.

"Grant 'Slider' McRae," Fork said and shook his head. "He is gonna be pissed we didn't call before now."

"He can't be," Creed said. "I tried calling four years ago when she was hurt and he said he didn't want to know, before I had even told him the situation."

"What a fucking prick," Harmony said. "Wait, I remember him, wasn't he one of the guys from your unit?"

"Yep, joined us when he got out. Stayed here for six months and then went to the Cali chapter," Creed said and she nodded, she did remember him, he was badass biker—scary too.

*****

Alive, Harmony thought, *Shady was alive and she was going to be fine.* Of course, she was going to be a pain in the ass for a few weeks. The doctor said she would be released in a week. The gunshot wound had hit her in the chest but had surprisingly missed everything important. Other than hurting like a son of a bitch, she was going to be fine.

Harmony walked out of the hospital with her two men beside her. They had brought her a change of clothes and she looked like a bag lady but her best friend was alive and she was fine. Creed and Fork promised her they would rain down the fires of hell on whoever did this. Lola and Dominic were going to die, and they were going to be the ones to kill them. Harmony had already called her shot.

In the biking world, calling a shot meant one of two things. Either you were in the circle of people to beat someone or you were in the circle of people to fire a shot at someone when they were executed.

She had never in her life thought she would actually call a shot for anyone. She knew about the rule, but thought she was too squeamish to carry it out. After looking into the eyes of a monster, she knew now what she had to do. Sometimes it was worth making a deal with the devil if the person wasn't worth the ink on the paper. She would take her shot, and then she was going to forget about it and scrape it off, because neither of those assholes deserved a second thought.

*****

Harmony sat in the police station after leaving the hospital. She wanted to go home but she had to answer questions first. The detective sitting across from her apparently didn't have a sense of humor, because after she told her story, the man just stared at her.

She refused to back down so she stared back.

"Just because you work for the DA doing investigations, and he is your daddy, does not mean you can do whatever the fuck you want in this town. Office building being burnt down. Stabbing a man with a fucking spork!" the man exploded.

"I didn't set the fire, and he was trying to kidnap me!" she yelled back, refusing to feel bad about that.

"Now you and your friend are shot, in what appears to be a hit being carried out, a bomb was strapped to your boyfriend's club and you waltz in here like it is a normal fucking day!" the detective continued.

"It is not a normal day, it is a shit day, why don't you go out and find the fuck head who shot me and my friend. I gave you his name, his description, and who he was with.

Find one of the little gangbangers and get the information out of him. I have no idea other than my company investigating a case why these assholes are targeting me."

They went round and round for an hour before Creed finally insisted on taking her home. She was winding down fast and her arm was throbbing. The bad part was she wasn't done for the day because her father was waiting for her when they pulled up.

"Daddy," she said and walked to him and he hugged her.

"Hey, honey," he whispered. Her father had come to the hospital to make sure Shady and she were fine and then he left. His office was calling in the big dogs to help, they had no choice, and Creed wasn't happy about that. Dominic Reyes III was a wanted man, so Fish was calling in favors to get some help.

"What is the word?" Creed asked.

Fish pulled back and kissed her on the forehead, then turned and said, "I called the authorities in Mexico and I am waiting for the warrant. He is wanted on murder, extortion, and trafficking drugs. They want him about as bad as we do, they are sending someone over."

"How long do we have?" Creed said.

"I can hold them off for a while, getting them set up; make sure there are no bodies and we are good," Fish shrugged.

"You got it," Fork said and together they took Harmony into their house.

Chapter Fourteen

She was home, Shady thought, and looked around the room Harmony had insisted on putting her in. The same room she had moved into when they left the main clubhouse. Home, the first one she had lived in since she left her family's home. FUCK, she was not thinking about that right now. She couldn't.

All she could think about was what Fork and Creed had just told her. Slider was coming back, and for her. Well, not for her, exactly, but to help take care of the situation with Dom. She didn't know how to deal with that, but she would have plenty of time to do it because she wasn't going anywhere.

Fuck, her heart couldn't take much more, she thought and looked out the window. But this was her family; Harmony wouldn't let anything happen to her, she knew it. The little biker bitch had been like a rabid dog this last week. Shady had teased her and laughed every single time she had snapped at one of the guys to get their asses moving.

She laughed when she heard the yelling, yeah she was home, but shit was going to fucking suck.

*****

Harmony slammed the door to their room behind her before the men could enter, stomping into the master bedroom, muttering the whole time. This was a shitty day. She had finally gotten Shady to lay still long enough without bitching, to help her with a routine. When she practiced a little while Shady had still been the hospital, the hospital staff had loved it. So she borrowed one of Shady's outfits, a hot one, a red leather bikini with snaps. She had taken the time to fucking do up her hair even though her arm was still bandaged and hurt because she wanted them to fuck her again. It had been a whole week, the fucking bastards. All she had heard was 'no babe, not until the doc okays it'. She was going to scream; today she thought she could force their hand. They had been ready to go into church and Freedom had done her routine for the club, so she figured why not her.

"Stupid, arrogant males who think they can tell me what to do and shit," Harmony said and then glared over her shoulder when Creed and Fork walked into the door.

"Woman, you should calm the hell down," Creed yelled.

Fork put his hand up to his face and rolled his eyes. This was seriously going to suck. "Cree…"

"What did you say?" Harmony yelled and pointed a finger at herself. "Look at this, it took me two fucking hours to look like this for you, and you have the nerve to bark at me to cover myself, like I looked like shit. I seriously do not believe the shit that comes out of your mouth sometimes."

"You heard me, calm down. I told you to cover up because I didn't want any of those assholes to see what is Fork's and mine. OURS! You do not walk around here half dressed looking like that. You can wear that only in our bedroom, nowhere else. Shit, that is a stripping outfit, I yelled because I knew you were going to strip like Free had and that is so not fucking happening," Creed yelled.

"Clue the fuck in, asshole, I was dressing like this for you! I don't look like a fucking stripper, I look like a badass biker babe who was going to strip for her men, dumbass!" Harmony screamed.

Fork held up a hand and said, "Babe, we just don't want your tits hanging out like that, I mean damn, no one sees those babies, they belong to us. You gotta learn, babe, Free is Easy and Pokes, what she does is on them. You are ours, and we are the President and Vice President of the club and, babe, that means we are greedy and don't like to fucking share our woman with anyone."

"Shut up!" Harmony growled. "The point to this is I took my time to look like this and you fuckheads didn't even tell me I looked hot, no, asshole over here said 'COVER YOURSELF' like I was a fuckin' leper or something. Seriously? You guys are pricks."

"Now that was just hateful," Fork pouted. "Creed, I do believe she needs a lesson. What do you think?"

Creed grinned and nodded. "I think she needs a little discipline. She needs to know if she wants to dress like a badass biker stripper, she can do that for us in this room. No one is gonna be looking at my woman getting hard and thinking about her when they are whacking off."

"What the fuck are you talking about? There is work to be done, damn it. We have a situation that needs discussed, stop thinking with your little head," Harmony scoffed.

"I don't have a little head, sweetheart," Creed drawled and began to walk toward her. "Besides, you are already undressed, if you didn't want us to fuck this situation out, you should have stayed dressed. It has been a week since we have been in that body, not waiting anymore."

While she'd been looking away from him, Fork began undressing. His boots, jeans, and shirt lay on the floor. He stood beside her and nipped her earlobe. A zing went straight down to her pussy. "We just need you to behave while we sort this all out."

She tried to move away from him, but he held her chin tight, and his mouth captured hers for a deep kiss. A shiver of anticipation ran over her. Her hands started to push him away, but forgot what they were supposed to do. Her fingers brushed across the soft hair on his chest and teased his nipples.

Fork reached behind her to unsnap her bra. He pulled it over her head and off. Then he carried her to the bedroom and threw her to the middle of the bed, while she squealed and laughed—he was growling at her.

"See how much we want you. You want us. I can smell your desire. Your nipples are swollen with longing for me to tease them," Fork said and laughed when her eyes grew big as Creed joined him at the end of the bed.

Holy shit, they were dangerously fuckin' handsome. She couldn't stay mad when she was just as aroused as they apparently were. Damn fucking sexy bastards, this sucked, she wanted to stay mad. They had been assholes, and they had also tried to tell her she wasn't allowed in on the investigation of Dom and Lola for another week, they wanted to protect her, grr, not happening.

His words ratcheted the heat level inside her to on fire.

Fork straddled her body and looked down. She almost felt him touch her with his intense stare. "Pinch your nipples. I want to see you." Creed laid down next to them so he could watch.

"I wanna see it too, baby, now go on, before you add some more punishment to your total," Creed said huskily. He kissed her passionately before pulling back and waiting.

Fork's command had her shivering with excitement. Her hands cupped her breasts while her thumbs stroked her nipples. All the muscles below her waist clenched tight as she watched his eyes turn to liquid silver. She turned her head and looked at Creed who was staring intently at her fingers.

"Move one hand down and grip my cock," Fork's husky voice brushed across her skin like warm silk. She gripped him firmly and began to move her hand up and down. The muscles of his face drew taut with desire.

"Oh, sweetheart, you are fuckin' amazing. Creed, her hand has the magic touch still."

Fork leaned down to her chest and brushed her hand aside. His mouth covered her taut nipple and sucked on her breast. Like a line pulling tight, she felt the tug in her pussy. Harmony could feel all of her thoughts leaving her head except for the one that mattered, *YES*! He went back and forth between each breast, giving each one attention.

Harmony rubbed across the top of his cock again as he paid his attention to her breasts, along the sensitive underside her finger glided slowly, teasing him a little like he was her. He groaned and his tongue flickered around and over her nipple more quickly.

Fork raised his head and caught her chin in his warm hand.

"I love you, I do. There is nothing in this world I would not do for you, including protect your crazy ass even when you don't need it. We need it. I need you to be safe, without you there *is* no us," he said huskily. "I'll stop now if you want, and we can talk, or you can tell me to continue."

His impassioned words speared through her heart. Turn back? Her body throbbed with need and burned with the fire he'd kindled inside her. She was wet with the juice from her desire. Her pussy lips ached to clamp around his hard cock. She tried to think clearly, but her mind screamed to take him inside her.

She pulled his head down close to her lips. "Take me, damn you, what the fuck do you think I was trying to get you to do?" she whispered the words.

He bit her lower lip and whispered back, "Anything to please my badass biker mama." He spread her legs wide and plunged deep. Her body arched with the intense pleasure. She pulled his hips tighter, pulling him in even more. All the time an unseen wire connected their eyes.

"Is that all you've got?" she taunted him.

"Damn you." His sizzling grin sent a tremor of response rippling across her skin. Pulling her legs up to his wide shoulders, he sank as deep as he could go. Then just as suddenly, he moved out. He bent his head to suck her clit and taste her sweet honey. His mouth and teeth teased, tasted, and sucked all along her pink folds and across her nub.

Harmony screamed for him to take her, but he only laughed and continued to torment her, bringing her to the edge, backing down, and then doing it again. Finally, when she thought she'd explode, he moved to her opening and slid back in. This time he moved slow and easy. Her pussy clamped around him, and her inner muscles trembled against his hot cock.

"I love you, sweetheart," he said as he went in all the way, and she split apart with the deep ecstasy of her orgasm. From a distance, she heard his shout of release.

"You two are having too much fun without me," Creed grumbled.

Harmony managed to turn her head in the direction of Creed. He was showing the softer side of himself since he had a pouting look on his face.

Fork rolled off her and smiled across at his brother. "It's your fault for being so mean," he spoke between gasping for breath. "She," he said, and nodded at Harmony, "and I haven't come to an understanding yet, you're welcome to join us, we need to make our point clear."

"No. I—"

Both men stared at her, but Creed said and then rolled closer to her and pinched one of her nipples, making her squirm. "You were saying, darling'?"

"You can't fuck me into submission," Harmony said stubbornly.

"Sure we can." Fork had moved over and pulled her with him. Creed leaned down and kissed her. "Sweetest kisser I've ever known."

"And I'm sure you've known quite a few," Harmony said sarcastically.

Creed looked across her to Fork. "I love her smart mouth." His lips covered hers again, and his hand moved down along her neck to her breast. He barely brushed the palm of his hand over the tip of her nipple.

She didn't think her body could move after what she'd just experienced with Fork, but her breast seemed to swell right in his hand, and a sizzle went straight to her pussy. His tongue slid inside her mouth and licked along the top and sides. She hadn't realized she'd turned toward him until she felt Fork's hands rubbing her back and cupping her backside. His lips nuzzled at her neck.

Their sexy scents and warm bodies enveloped her, and her head and body responded immediately. Her every nerve more sensitive than they'd ever been to a touch or a kiss. Her insides wept with moisture. She felt her pussy pulse with a craving to have one of their hot, hard cocks inside her.

Creed's mouth traveled down her body. At the juncture to her thighs, he separated her pink folds and rubbed his thumb across her clit. She moaned. Fork had moved to her breasts and suckled one while he teased the nipple of the other. A tremor started inside her pussy and traveled to every nerve. She had a voracious hunger for her two men that both thrilled and frightened her.

Her legs were spread wider. Creed quickly lined up and placed his cock at the entrance to her pussy. He began to move in slowly as Fork kissed her mouth, and moved his tongue in and out to match Creed's rhythm below. Fork still rubbed across her taut nipples and Harmony was sure at any moment she'd explode with the tension building inside her.

"Let go, sweetheart." She heard Fork's voice in her ear. Creed moved faster and deeper, and a tide of pleasure shook her and sent her over the edge. She heard Creed groan out his release.

The inner walls of her pussy clenched around his cock and held as soft ripples continued to roll through her. She savored the feeling of being held close in their embrace, a warm, sexy cocoon to rest in and catch her breath. But as she did, reality intruded.

"See how nice we are, now, let's talk about your blatant disregard of our need to protect you," Creed said, flipping her so quickly she felt dizzy. He smoothed his hand over her ass and she yelled.

"Don't you dare, I swear on all that is holy, if you spank me I am gonna kick your ass."

Chapter Fifteen

Slider rode his bike into town, he looked to the right and grinned at the man who rode with him. This was going to cause a serious clusterfuck but he didn't care. Ryan 'Cajun' Dubois needed the club and the club needed him, it was time for him to come home. He hadn't contacted Creed and Fork when he got out a year ago; instead, he had come to Cali and stayed with him. Injured in a roadside bomb, Cajun was fucked up in the head for six months. He hadn't wanted to speak to his previous buddies that were in his unit. He was squared away now, although his old smiling good Louisiana sense of humor wasn't there anymore, in its place was a cold-hearted bastard. One that Slider knew the club needed right now.

He was supposed to be here two weeks ago, but two weeks ago he had a contract that needed fulfilling for another charter. It was too important to put off and so he had told Creed he would be late, his Prez had not been happy.

That was going to sting, and he knew it. Cajun had avoided all of their phone calls, not answering a single one. His mother called to inform him Creed and Fork were threatening to hunt his ass down if he didn't answer the phone. She didn't know where he was either, but at least he answered the phone to her.

Slider had understood what the guy had been going through, he had been injured as well, but not as severely. The scars on his back were his only reminder of the time he had been held prisoner for a week.

It had fucked him in the head, and seriously, he hadn't cared. He also knew because of that he had also fucked Shady over, something he was sorry about but he couldn't change. She deserved better than him and he wasn't going back there to rekindle anything. He was going back to figure out what the fuck was going on and to protect her ass.

Slider motioned for Cajun to pull into the remote storage area they were supposed to be meeting Easy and Poke. It had been a year since the guys had come to Cali on a run, but they knew how he worked, and he knew how they did. This place was their place to take people they needed to talk. The storage area belonged to the club, and they used it for their mine, and for members to put their shit if they needed it.

Slider had one. When he left there, he had put everything he had in storage. But that wasn't why they were there. They were there to make some stupid son of a bitch talk. They heard the idiot had tried to take Creed and Fork's woman in a Starbucks and she had stabbed him with a spork, it had been hilarious when recounted. Slider was a cleaner, and it didn't mean he actually cleaned, it meant if there was some situation that needed to be cleaned up he did it. No matter if it was to take care of a body, provide alibis, new papers for people to disappear, or torture information out of someone until they were no longer useful. He was a stone cold killer and Cajun was just like him.

The guy was released from the hospital two weeks ago and Easy and Poke had just caught up to him, they needed his expertise to get him to talk. So far, every single one of these bastards refused to give them any information that actually mattered. This asshole was farther up the food chain they discovered. He had to know more, and if he did—Slider was going to find out.

As they pulled into the drive, Slider frowned. Shit, Creed and Fork were there as well. As they pulled up, Creed stepped forward. Cajun got off his bike and pulled his helmet off. He could see the confusion on his President's face, but then it cleared and his face went rock hard. Fuckin' A.

"Creed," Slider said and nodded, but his leader only had eyes for Cajun. Fork stepped out of the storage shed and his mouth dropped open, yep, completely fucked up situation.

No one moved. A female walked out of the shed who drew his attention next. *Damn, she was gorgeous*, Slider thought. Strawberry blonde hair, wearing a black tank top, black jeans, and black biking boots. She had a bandage of her arm but he could tell she was fit, her muscles defined.

"Hey, honey," the woman said and draped her arm over Creed's shoulder. *Shit, this was Harmony? She didn't look the same,* was his first thought.

"Yeah, babe," Creed said.

"Who is this?" she said, staring at Cajun, her eyes slid to him and he lifted his chin.

"Slider," Creed said.

"I know that, babe," Harmony said.

Cajun stepped forward and met his previous leader toe to toe. Harmony did not step back, she did not flinch, and she did not smile and give him a greeting. Instead, she stared at the man intently and waited. Slider respected that, because he knew what Cajun's eyes looked like, he also knew the scar running down the side of his face was not pretty. Most women looked away.

"I can't be sure," Creed said slowly. "Looks like a guy who used to be in my unit. But it can't be him because he has refused to take my calls, babe. Since he refused to take my calls, I can only assume he wanted nothing to do with what we were offering, which was a place in the Warriors. It also can't be him because Slider would never bring someone onto my territory that has not taken my calls and refused the offer I gave him, because in doing so would get his ass kicked from here to the fucking state line and back again."

"Oh," Harmony said slowly. "And what is the name of the man this can't be?"

"Cajun," Creed said slowly.

"'Cause he likes spicy food?" she asked.

"No, 'cause his momma is a voodoo queen," Creed said.

"Would come in handy," Harmony said.

"Maybe," Creed said.

Then there was silence again and Cajun finally spoke. "Creed…"

"Fuck that, asshole," Fork said and walked to his friend and cuffed him up the side of his head. "Only need a yes or no."

"Yes," Cajun said and Creed nodded then his gaze swung to me.

"We will discuss this later." Slider nodded and looked at Harmony who was now grinning.

"Hey, we have someone we want you to meet."

Slider raised an eyebrow to his leaders; women weren't usually witnesses to what he did. He wasn't sure he was comfortable with it.

"I stabbed him with a spork," Harmony said dryly. "I am pretty sure that I can handle this."

Slider still waited, Creed needed to give him the go-ahead. When he nodded slightly, Slider walked slowing into the shed. A man was tied to the chair and bleeding from his mouth and his face was bruised.

"Who started on him?" Slider said softly.

He expected Easy or Poke who were the enforcers to say it was them, but when there was more silence, he turned and looked. Harmony was looking up at the ceiling and refused to meet anyone's eyes. Finally she snapped.

"Fine, it was me, I got bored, and seriously, the fucker ruined my Starbucks experience, it will never be the same," she yelled.

"She normal?" Cajun asked quietly.

"You did not just say that," Harmony yelled and glared at him.

"Has an anger management issue, working on fucking it out of her, but so far she's holding on," Creed said and Harmony glared at him as well.

"Oh really?" she huffed.

"Babe, told you, mouth shut, and ears open, your crew runs the investigation, I get the information, that is it," Creed said and Fork covered his mouth because he was trying not to laugh.

"Oh really?" she snorted.

"Really," Fork said and then they waited. It had to be some weird game they were playing, Slider decided, because the three of them were looking like they were going to tear each other's clothes off.

Easy rolled his eyes. "You get used to their foreplay, it is twisted."

For the first time in a year, Cajun laughed. Slider turned with a surprised look on his face and stared at his friend. "Don't think you're fuckin' your woman hard enough, boss."

"See, told you," Harmony smirked and Slider shook his head.

"You got anything to say?" Slider asked the man who was tied to the chair, glaring at them as well.

"*Chupame la verga*," the man spit out.

Harmony snorted. "He said suck his dick."

"You understand him?" Slider said, never moving his eyes off the man's face.

"Yep." She laughed and Slider shrugged.

"Not sucking your dick. Anything else to say?" Slider said.

"*Jodete!*" the man said with a sneer.

Harmony snorted. "Told you to go fuck yourself."

Slider nodded and Cajun moved, he had helped him with his last job as well and knew how Slider worked. He could feel Creed's hesitation with using Cajun but he didn't interrupt.

Cajun grabbed a towel from the table, wrapped it around the man's head and pulled him back so he was laying on his back in the chair, the back resting on Cajun's leg.

Slider picked up the hose from the corner and turned on the water. He pointed the stream over the man's face and waited.

Slider had learned this trick in the military—waterboarding was a useful tool. The man tried to turn his head, push the air out but it didn't work, it never did. The towel soaked up the moisture and held it in so when he tried to breath it went into his lungs.

Slider left on the water for a few minutes and then turned it off. He nodded and Cajun let the guy go and the chair tipped forward quickly. The man began coughing and trying to puke up the water.

He pulled a cigarette out of his pocket and shook one out. While he waited for the guy to get a breath, he lit the smoke. The burn of the tar in his lungs felt good.

Slider stepped in front of the guy and said, "Got anything to say?" and blew a stream of smoke into his face.

"*Chingada Madre*," the man choked.

"Called you a muther fucker," Harmony said in a toneless voice. Slider was impressed, he expected her voice to be shaky and shit, like most chicks would sound like when they saw him waterboarding anyone. Her eyes showed nothing, she had locked it down, *impressive*.

Slider nodded again and Cajun repeated wrapping his head again and tipping him back. On and on he went, torturing the dude, asking questions until the fucker finally broke. It took five hours, but Harmony had gone and gotten McDonalds. It had been their break while the dude actually passed out.

"Any of that make sense?" Slider asked, cleaning his hand from slitting the guy's throat when he had finally spilled.

"Yeah," Creed sighed. "Church in the morning."

"Be there, what about Cajun?" Slider asked.

Creed and Fork were silent, they had shit to work out but Creed nodded and Fork nodded as well. "Bring him to the compound, we will talk in the morning about him too."

"Cool," Slider said and turned. "Cajun, we gotta clean up."

Cajun waved and pulled out a tarp and laid it on the ground. Creed and the others left, but not before Harmony went to stand over the body and stared down at it. With a shake of her head, she turned and walked away. The roar of the motorcycles wasn't a distraction to the two men, they had a job to do, and they did it well.

Chapter Sixteen

Creed looked at Harmony who had come out of the shower after they got home, and he frowned. Fork had come down to tell him she asked for time alone, he didn't like it. If she needed to talk to them, they would listen, it was the only way this would all work.

"Babe," he said as she walked into the room wrapped in a towel.

Harmony sighed and put her head down. She just needed a few to process shit, sometimes she got a little worried when stuff she did and saw didn't bother her. She wondered if there was something wrong with her.

"Creed," she tried to smile.

"What is going on in that head of yours?" Creed said and Fork walked into the room and leaned against the wall.

"Nothing," she said and went to the dresser and grabbed some clean underwear and suddenly Creed was there, grabbing her and forcing her to look at him.

"Babe," he said forcefully.

"Fine," she grumbled. "I think I am a psychopath."

Creed froze and Fork burst out with a laugh and she looked around Creed's shoulders and frowned.

"What the fuck, babe." He laughed.

"It didn't bother me," she argued and Creed smiled down at her.

"What didn't," he said.

"Torturing that guy. I didn't feel a damn thing," she huffed and looked up at him and frowned. "Most women would have been freaked out."

"And?" Creed laughed. "You are not most women, babe."

"I know that," she said sarcastically.

"If you were most women you wouldn't be our woman. Because, babe, we live in a world where black and white are shades of gray. Shit is not nice; in fact, it is fucking awful.

We see the worst of the worst because of who we are. You grew up here, it isn't right or wrong, it just is. The only thing you need to remember is that you can love, and your love is fierce, loyal, and true. Psychopaths do not love."

Harmony was quiet and tried to mull it over in her head. It still bothered her. "Will you tell me if I begin to go down that path."

Fork moved and pulled her to stand in front of him and looked down. "Babe, we are your anchor, you are ours. That is how this works, if you ever think you are floating out there, then come to us and we will pull you back. But never think you are alone. We will always be the ones who pull you back."

"That sounds nice," she said.

However, she was about to pull away, but before she could, Fork's arms wrapped around her, and he pulled her to him, crushing her against his hard body, and he started to devour her lips like a man starving. His tongue pushed against the seam of her lips, and she opened, willingly, allowing him to sweep in and mingle his tongue with hers. She didn't know which one of them groaned when their tongues met, him or her, or maybe both, all she knew was she was getting drunk off his taste and didn't want him to stop. One of his hands found the back of her head, and pinned her in place while he assaulted her mouth with his tongue. The other ran down her body until it cupped her ass under her towel and pressed her against his hard length.

"I love your fucking body," Fork stated as he pulled from her mouth to trail kisses down her jaw.

She couldn't form a coherent answer to the statement because, at the moment, Fork was rubbing her soaked mound against his erection, hidden behind the zipper of his jeans, making her dizzy from the hot trail his mouth was leaving.

Creed turned her suddenly and the onslaught from his mouth began until she was breathless. Fuck, they knew how to get to her, make her forget all of her worries, and make everything better.

She felt another set of hands grab her breasts from behind; she looked up at Creed and grinned. He turned her and sat down on the bed with her in his lap, legs spread over his knees, and whipped the towel off to the side. She was facing Fork now and smiled.

Her nipples were like diamonds at this point, so hard they hurt, and Fork began to tweak them, twisting and pulling them a bit. She groaned at the pain and pleasure sensations shooting from her breasts to her clit, and her pussy gushed fresh juices, soaking Creed's jeans.

Creed pulled her head to the side and leaned over her shoulder to watch what Fork was doing, and Harmony could see the desire burning in his eyes. The hand that was holding her head still came away and went to one of her large, heavy breasts and she felt one of Fork's hands go to the other. They worked her together and she leaned her head back and rested it on Creed's shoulder giving them both access.

Creed just watched his hand and Fork's hand fondle, pinch, pull, and tease her breasts and nipples, and Harmony went frantic with need for him or Fork to do more, while she writhed and moaned on his lap. Suddenly she was flipped and facing him, straddling him. With Fork behind her running his hands down her back.

"God, you're beautiful, Harmony," Creed said reverently. "I love your tits."

She didn't have time to respond to his words because in seconds he was leaning over and taking one of her nipples into his mouth. She moaned loudly, her body shaking, as Creed's hot mouth suckled her tender nipple before he bit down on it and then licked the sting away with his tongue.

She thought for a second how talented he was with his mouth, she could lay here forever and let them touch her, but the thought flew out of her head when she felt Creed's hand slide between their bodies to tickle her clit.

When his finger made contact with her sensitive clit, she almost shot off his lap. However, Fork held her down with a chuckle.

Creed's fingers glided through her slick folds, and he groaned around her nipple, sending tingling feelings all over her body. A finger pushed into her pussy, while his thumb began to rub circles around her clit.

Harmony was on fire. The feeling of both men touching her intimately, was burning her alive. This was her life now, and she was never going to let this go, damn but she loved them.

Fork pulled her head back by her hair and kissed her passionately. She noticed he wasn't wearing a shirt anymore, and when he pressed his body to hers, pushing her mound against Creed's hand and cock, she could feel that Fork wasn't wearing anything else either. His wide, stiff cock pressed against her bottom, nothing keeping them from touching completely skin to skin.

"Damn it, I need to fuck this ass," Fork proclaimed, frustrated. "Stand up for a minute, babe, and Creed can get undressed too. I am about to fucking blow already."

She stood and smiled, running her hands down Fork's body and touching him everywhere. He moaned and lifted his head to the ceiling. She loved having this power over them.

Then Creed turned to look at her with his hand stretched out to her, "Come here, baby." He had shed his clothes and was standing by the bed looking like a badass biker that he was.

She bit her lip, and ran her tongue over her lips, she wanted to taste them again, and she craved it. With a little twitch in her hips she went to Creed. His eyes got darker as he watched her. As if he couldn't wait, he took a step, scooped her up, and walked back to the bed, whispering in her ear, "Fuck, babe, you mouth is tempting."

He sat down with her once again on his lap and kissed her gently. Slowly sweeping his tongue into her mouth and caressing hers. Damn it, she hated it when he went sweet, then she was going to have to be sweet as well.

Fork pressed into her from behind again, kissing her shoulders, her neck, and her back, as he wrapped his arms around her and massaged her breasts.

Creed rubbed his rigid length between her pussy lips, hitting her clit, and making her whimper into his mouth. He pulled away from her lips, trailing hot kisses down her jaw to her ear, and bit on her lobe before he suckled it.

"You're so wet for us, baby," he whispered into her ear. "I can't wait to fuck this tight cunt."

"Please, yes," she begged, but Creed seemed content with just torturing her for the moment, as he continued to just rub himself against her slowly.

"Our babe likes to beg," Fork said. "By the time we are done, babe, you will be desperate for our cocks."

"I already am, I need it hard and fast," she protested, and Creed suddenly stopped moving to look at her, with a stormy expression on his face.

"You don't tell us how to give you our cock," Fork answered in a hard tone and she shivered, not even noticing Creed's face. "We give it to you how we want to."

Creed just looked at her for a moment, gloating, and then a smile spread across his face, "We own this body."

"Well, you could start by fucking it," she stated firmly.

He and Creed chuckled before Fork spoke, "Creed, lay down. Harmony, climb up and sit on Creed's face."

Her face heated with desire at his command. Creed shuffled underneath her to lie down, and she hesitated, not sure she should do what Fork said. They couldn't boss her around all the time.

Fork laughed at her and slapped her ass hard and then said. "Babe, don't make us wait for this shit. Haven't you learned?"

"No," she laughed.

She let Creed and Fork guide her into position on Creed's shoulders, and looked down at Creed, who flashed her a sexy smile.

"Lean forward, and put your hands against the head board," Fork instructed, and she complied, shutting her eyes.

Creed wrapped his arms around her thighs and pulled her further, up, making her squeak, but before she could protest, his tongue came out and licked her pussy, causing her to jump. His arms kept her in place, he continued his assault, licking her from her center to her clit, and she relaxed into his embrace.

As he got more vigorous, lapping at her slit, circling her clit, and stabbing his tongue into her center, she forgot all about her need to get it hard and fast and found herself pushing into his face, trying to get closer.

Then he went back to eating her as if she were his last meal ever.

She looked over her shoulder to see Fork holding out his cock, and she moaned as she opened her mouth and allowed him to sink in.

Harmony tried to concentrate, but Creed was pushing her closer and closer to the edge, and she was dizzy with desire. She closed her eyes, then reached down with one hand to grab Creed's hair as she rode his face, and he thrust his tongue into her core over and over. Then held onto Forks thigh as he fucked her face. She lost track of time as she just felt. Fork tasted amazing, and she closed her mouth around his cock and swallowed on one of his passes. They were owning her, she loved it.

Finally, Creed rolled his tongue against her clit, flicking it, and rolling it, and she shot over the edge, screaming Creed's name around Fork's cock, as her body broke apart and her pussy spasmed. Creed stabbed his tongue into her center, collecting her come as it poured out of her, and feeling her vaginal walls constrict around his tongue trying to milk it, and she soared in the sky, never wanting to fall down again. Fork pulled out of her mouth with a pop and moved.

Fork picked her up and scooted her down Creed's body, where Creed held his cock ready for her. Her cunt was still pulsing from the orgasm.

However, Fork held her up slightly as Creed made slow, shallow thrusts up, pushing himself into her an inch at a time. *Shit, this was fucking hot*.

Once Creed was inside, he held her hips still as she adjusted. For the longest time, they all just sat there, not moving, and Harmony began to grow impatient.

She wiggled her hips, trying to get them to do something, and Creed groaned loudly.

"Now *fuck* me," she growled

Fork chuckled behind her and Creed said, "As my woman wishes."

Creed held her hips, and lifted her up slightly then brought her back down hard. His cock rubbed against every nerve ending inside of her, and her body tingled with renewed arousal. He picked her up and brought her down again, and she moaned as her body began to burn all over with pleasure as she found her rhythm. Fork took her breasts as she rode Creed.

Creed thrust up into her as she came down, and each time they connected her stomach coiled tighter and tighter. She felt the love, the connection.

Fork tapped on her clit and she flew over the edge again, coming apart on top of Creed. She felt paralyzed by pleasure, but Creed continued to pummel into her, until he pushed deep inside of her, yelling her name and succumbing to the same paralysis. She could feel her pussy milking his cock as he shot his load into her.

Before she had an opportunity to recover from her orgasm, she found herself lying on her back beside Creed, and Fork blanketing her. She wondered for a moment if she would be able to come again, but as he began to kiss her hungrily, she started to feel her body become aroused again, she realized she would.

"Forgive me, baby," Fork said, looking down at her. "This is going to be hard and fast. I'll make it up to you, but I've been waiting to be inside you."

She saw his need and couldn't help but smile, "Just fuck me, Fork."

He didn't wait to be told twice. With one swift thrust, he was deep inside her, stretching her more than Creed had. Then he started to move. He powered in and out of her, going deep and hard, and she couldn't get enough of him.

He sat back on his feet, bringing her hips up with his hands under her butt, and guided his cock in and out of her. The new angle pushed against something inside of her, making her body hum and her belly tighten again.

She felt a hot mouth cover her nipple and looked down to find Creed licking and biting her breast. He reached his hand out to pinch and pull on the other one as he suckled on her nipple, the sensations shot down to her pussy, making it spasm around Fork's cock.

He groaned and thrust harder, "Fuck, Creed, don't stop playing with her breasts."

For what seemed like forever, Fork fucked her, as Creed played with her breasts, and she writhed and begged them for more. Her body was wound up tighter than it had ever been before and she thought she was about to die.

Finally, Creed slipped his hand down to pinch her clit, and then she shattered into a million pieces, taking a roaring Fork with her. They both froze after Fork plunged one last time into her, spraying her pussy with his come.

Fork rolled to flop down on the other side of her, and Creed rested his head on her breast, as Fork turned to her and wrapped an arm around her middle, while resting his head on his other arm.

Creed moved his head away after a few minutes, and Harmony missed the weight of him, so she turned on her side and placed her head on his shoulder as Fork touched her back.

"Love you," Creed said, after moments of silence.

Harmony opened her eyes, "I know."

"Love you too," Fork whispered.

"Duh" she said and closed her eyes. *They loved her crazy*, she thought and she drifted off to sleep.

Chapter Seventeen

If there was anything in this world Shady hated, it was sleeping alone. But sleeping alone meant she was going to have nightmares. When she had someone in her bed she trusted, like any one of the Warriors, they kept them at bay. They were her own personal knights in shining armor. She loved them for that, and she wasn't embarrassed to use them to keep her safe.

The nightmares didn't come every single time she slept alone, they did a sneak attack. Shady learned over the years she could have two or three days in between someone sleeping with her before they returned. It had been a week and four days since she had been in the hospital and every night she slept alone. The nightmares were only getting worse.

They always started the same because in real life it had started that way. Dominic wasn't her full brother, he was her stepbrother, not that it made a difference because her mother would never make that distinction. Because in doing so would mean she wasn't the love of Dominic Reyes II life. Her mother would never allow herself to think that.

Shady had no idea who her real father was, and she didn't care. Her mother never allowed her to question her husband's claim to be her father, and so at five when her mother married Dominic Reyes II, Francesca became a Reyes, and that meant, she was family.

Form the moment Shady and her mother moved onto the estate, Dominic had his eye on her. It made her shiver every single time when she remembered their first introduction. He was ten years older than her so at fifteen, he seemed larger than life. He scared her, and he knew it. Instead of most people who would try to put a child at ease, Dom thrived on her fear; in fact, when she finally ran away she had come to realize he not only thrived on her fear—he actually craved it. It was an addiction like no other.

The first time he came to her room in the dead of night, she had been twelve. Blossoming into womanhood, just beginning to learn about boys and he had taken that away from her. Fuck, he had taken a lot more than that away from her. Thus the nightmares, because after the first time where Dominic told her that she was his and his alone, he proceed to make sure she understood it.

Her mother never questioned Dom's possessive behavior toward her; she always just said 'your brother loves you'. But love had nothing to do with what Dominic Reyes felt and did to her. That was sick and twisted and Shady ran from those memories all of her life. But apparently she didn't run far enough, because he was here and she was going to have to face him. This time though, she wasn't going to face him alone.

The first night, she woke Harmony with her screams. Her friend came into her room and checked on her, assuming the nightmare was from the shooting no doubt. The second night, she stayed a little longer and this time Fork came in with her because he had been getting a drink of water and heard her scream. But the third night, it was bad, real bad, and that night her friends would be the only thing that would keep her from jumping off the ledge of sanity, and it was also the night they would understand what they were up against.

"You are mine," Dominic always said when he walked into her room.

Shady whimpered from the bed, she couldn't help it, whenever he came into her room she knew the pain that was coming.

"Get up," he ordered and Shady quickly left her small twin bed and stood before him, if she delayed there would be consequences.

"Why are you wearing that nightgown? I have told you what I want you to wear to bed," he yelled and ripped her nightgown right down the front. Shady hated his silky nighties he wanted her to wear; she could barely touch them anymore. Tonight, when she had gone to bed, she knew

what she was doing, but she couldn't bring herself to put on one of his presents. Instead, she wore the nightgown her grandmother had sent her.

She stood before him, shivering, only in her panties and Dominic grinned at her. She hated that look; it meant it was going to hurt.

He grabbed her arm and dragged her to the bathroom where he always made her shower before and after he was done with her. Shady stumbled and almost fell but Dom had a grip on her arm. Angrily he turned and raised his hand…

She screamed, she knew she did because she also dreamed this was the night he had almost broken her. The night she realized she had to get away.

"Shady," Harmony whispered from the doorway. Shady wasn't awake, she was in that mid stage of half awake and half asleep, where you couldn't escape.

"No more," she screamed and thrashed against the blankets.

Creed and Fork had followed Harmony tonight, it was getting worse. Harmony knew something was going to have to give with her friend because she couldn't keep living like this. Every night waking from the nightmares that haunted her, it was a miracle that she was sane.

Harmony went to the bed and tried to grab her friend and hold onto her. Shady fought her like a mad woman. Screaming and fighting her like her life depended on it. It had, but Creed and Fork never knew the extent to what these dreams meant until tonight.

"I am not your woman," Shady scream and fought Harmony. Creed and Fork stood helplessly by as they watched their friend battle some unknown force.

"Shady!" Harmony snapped and pulled her arms down. "Wake up, honey."

"I will never be," Shady screamed and fought harder.

Creed stepped forward like he was going to help Harmony and Fork grabbed his arm and shook his head and whispered, "You could make it worse."

"Worse than this?" Creed whispered.

"Listen to what she is saying, man, she is fighting a guy," Fork whispered and Creed nodded.

They listened to the heart wrenching cries from their friend and watched their woman try to calm her. Shady wouldn't wake up though. Finally, Harmony had wrapped her arms around her friend, crawled into bed with her, wrapped her legs around her as well, and held on.

The two women thrashed and moved on the bed until finally Shady settled down. They thought she was awake and maybe she was a little but she wasn't fully or she would never have shared what she did with them.

"Harmony," Shady whispered in a broken almost childlike voice.

"Yeah, honey," Harmony whispered back.

"I can't go back there," Shady said with a sob.

"I know," Harmony whispered.

"No you don't," Shady said. "I will kill myself before that happens."

"Honey, what did he do, get it out," Harmony whispered and both men stiffened and froze, they didn't want to hear this, but they had to.

"I was twelve the first time he came to me, God, I thought I was going to die it hurt so bad," Shady whispered. "He said I was his, he loved me, he was the only one who would ever love me like that because I was his precious gift. My God, Harmony, he was sick. For a while I prayed for death. I thought my mother was going to help me when she knew, I told her and she smiled and took my hand and said I was chosen for him, I should be happy. I freaked, they just shook their heads, and mother gave me a sedative to use at night. She said it would get better. It didn't, it got worse, he was sick and depraved and he took me right along with him into hell."

"Aww, honey," Harmony whispered and held her tighter.

Creed and Fork listened, and with each word out of her mouth, they became angrier. Shady was part of their family, her pain was theirs, and right now, she held a lot of pain.

"You know those demon masks you see all the time. That is him; he would look so much like those masks in the night. During the day he was a cocky bastard but at night, he was a monster, a demon," Shady whispered and then she let the story flow out of her. The whole thing.

    Harmony was sobbing with her friend, holding onto her and not letting go while Creed and Fork just stood there and listened. Toward the end, the men left, they had heard enough and Harmony cried with Shady as she finished her story and then they just stayed together and held each other the rest of the night and part of the next day. Harmony never left her friend's side, and she didn't search out her men, she was there for Shady.

Epilogue

Slider and Cajun buried the body in the desert and then drove back toward the compound. It was a beautiful morning, but it wouldn't stay that way.

As they rolled into the compound and got off their bikes, Creed and Fork came out front and they looked pissed.

"Church in five," Creed barked and Slider nodded. Something happened between last night and this morning.

Cajun walked to his side and shook his head. "No rest for the wary."

"Don't think we are going to have rest for a long time," Slider said.

They walked into the clubhouse and looked around. The guys were just now getting up and moving but they felt the air of tension. As they filed into the room where they held their meeting, Slider greeted several of the men, but they were staring at him with a hard expression, like he had done something wrong. He didn't know what.

"Dominic Reyes III is a dead man," Creed said with a hard tone. The room was silent as he began to speak and Slider lost it completely. It took five men to hold him down from leaving the compound and hunting for that bastard.

Finally, Slider got his answer, and it ripped him apart knowing he had once again failed someone who needed him.

He hadn't known, damn it.

Books by Harley McRide

Ops Warriors MC
Sharing Freedom
Bringing Harmony
Coming Soon: Book Three

Devil Savages MC
Bed of Roses
Coming Soon: Book Two

I would love to hear from you!

Website: http://harleymcride.webs.com/
Facebook: https://www.facebook.com/harley.mcride?fref=ts

Excerpt from Bed of Roses
Devil Savages MC Book One
By Harley McRide

Rose checked herself one last time in her rearview mirror, dabbing on a coat of lipstick before she headed into Devil's Den. She wasn't big on cosmetics, but had layered it on thick, complete with smoky eyes and red lipstick. Instead of the average girl next door that normally stared back at her, there was a hot woman she didn't recognize. She felt sexy and just the boost she needed to follow through and not hightail it back to the safety of her house. The parking lot was packed, making her park all the way out on the back forty on the grass. There were so many bikes it put Sturgis to shame. Row after row of pure American muscle filled most of the area, leaving the last few rows for cars and trucks. When she stepped out of the car, her heels sunk in the mud making walking almost impossible. By the time she hit pavement, her calves were burning and she was pretty sure there were blisters swelling up on her heels.

Great.

The roar of the crowd echoed out around her, amped up in bloodlust ready for the fights. The sounds clouded with the thick humidity making it hard to breathe. Rose sucked a gulp of the pollutant deep in her lungs to steady her nerves. She reached down and smoothed her clothing, thinking twice about her wardrobe choice, growing more and more apprehensive by the second. The little black leather mini skirt paired with black stilettos made her legs appear longer and leaner. She had chosen a pink tank top that dipped low in the front to accent her large chest and give an ample amount of cleavage without coming off too slutty. Standing there ready to face what waited ahead, she felt naked. Just as her nerves got the better of her and she was about to bolt, the door swung open. Rose looked up, staring at a towering Tonto.

Tonto looked down at the little brunette, doing a double take at what he saw. Not much rattled him. He was surrounded by willing and ready snatch every day, and yet this little vanilla cupcake sucked his attention better than Red sucked cock, which said a lot considering the little cunt could suck a golf ball through a water hose while being double fucked in the ass, and without dribbling a single drop. The innocent little mouse was decked out looking good enough to eat. "You're early. I'm surprised you showed." His eyes roamed over her, taking in every hot little curve and dip. His height gave him a perfect view down her cleavage, making his balls draw up painfully tight. *Fuck me. Where has this little sexy bitch been hiding?* As his eyes finally made their way down to her legs, it took a conscious amount of restraint to keep from pinning her up against the wall and shoving the little skirt up her hips. He could almost feel her cunt squeezing around his cock.

"I don't believe in being late. Thank you again for seeing me." She squared her shoulders, giving herself a false dose of confidence.

"You're good to see, baby." He held the door open for her, locking his eyes on her ass as she swayed in front of him. *Mmm. I might need to test out all her talents.*

Rose about tripped. Did Tonto, the President of the infamous Devil Savages, just flirt with her? She wanted to jump up and down, but despite looking like a total ass, she knew there was no way her tiny lace bra would keep the girls from bouncing out the top of her shirt. The moment she stepped through the doors, her senses went on overload. The walls were painted dark, leaving the main focal point the octagon ring in the middle of the stadium. On both sides were two semi-circle rows of seats, going up into the nosebleed section. People of all shapes and sizes were around her, dressed from business suits to tiny scraps of material barely covering nipple and crotch. The smell of alcohol and cigarettes invaded her nose making her sneeze. Her little 'achoo' came out in a squeak, getting an amused smirk from him over his shoulder. *How the hell did he hear it over the deafening music and screams that blare from all directions?* As they entered the main room, Rose was stopped by the crowd. Tonto took her hand and stepped forward, parting them like the Red Sea. People literally stepped on top of each other to get out of his way. She knew he was intimidating, but this was ridiculous. Girls jumped out at him from every direction, offering drinks and rubbing against him like bitches in heat. If she weren't so shell-shocked, she would have puked.

He led her to the back and up a narrow dim staircase that led into a long corridor. He unlocked the first door to their left and ushered her inside, shutting it behind them. Inside wasn't exactly what she was expecting. The flooring had black plush carpet that worked great with the blood red walls and black leather furniture. A huge flat screen television perched on the far wall, taking up the entire space. In the corner was a desk with a door directly behind it. It was…comfortable. "Have a seat." He waltzed over and plopped down on the couch, staring at her in wait. She jumped and scurried to the chair that sat opposite of him and sat on the edge, her body rigid and uptight. His stare lingered, penetrating her. The longer the silence dragged on, the more she seized up.

She couldn't stand it any longer. "Is there something I should be doing? I didn't see a fridge, but would you like something to drink?" He didn't answer. His grey eyes cut straight to her soul. *Why is he not talking? What did I do wrong? Please don't let this be one of those places that expects sexual favors. No job is worth that. I'll just have to double up hours at the diner…maybe I can get something down at the factory. Yeah, time to go…before this gets ugly.* "Look, I'm sorry for wasting your time. I can see that I'm not qualified for the job so I'll just be going now. Thanks again for your time." She stood and took a step toward the door when he finally broke his monk silence.

"Sit. Here." He pointed to the cushion next to him. The corners of his lips tilted up ever so slightly, breaking his stone-cold poker face. All of her radars went off at the same time. She had heard about people who had set up fake interviews and schemed the potential interviewees into participating in sexual acts then found it uploaded on the internet before they even got home. *Fuck to the no.* She was not going to be an amateur porn star, no matter how much money they promised. Her mother on the other hand would have jumped on the opportunity. Maybe she should pass the word…at least the woman would be helping with the bills. She kept her legs spread and was on her back most of the time anyway. Anger raged through Rose at not only the situation but her thoughts too. Had he heard about her mom? Is that why he called her in here? Fuck, her life was one huge white trash train wreck with no light at the end of the tunnel except the oncoming engine that threatened to plow her into hell. Whether it was pent up anger and hurt from the last twenty-three years of her existence or fear of never getting out and having a life, she exploded.

"Listen, I'm not sure what this is all about but I think there has been a misunderstanding. I came here for a job, not to fall on my knees and suck my way to the top. I was under the impression there was a legit position open that didn't require me turning into one of the whores who fall at your feet. I have five kids at home that all seem to think they need food, clothing, and a roof over their head. Have a *great* night."

Excerpt from Big Dog
Burning Bastards MC Book One
By Ryder Dane

    They were back, she felt them come in before she saw them. It was early in the afternoon, and she wanted to get things organized with Clementine before she went with the bikers. She knew they would find out she was the Oracle they were looking for and if she fought them, she might not get the chance to come back and resume her life here. If she went willingly, then they had to allow her to leave the club when she wished. Whatever they wanted from her, she wasn't playing party tricks anymore, and she planned to tell them that too. The fact Crazy Charlie hadn't recognized her yet was no surprise.
    He never spoke to her back in the day, back when he was one of the hardcore biker life type of men, he still wore his old-school colors over his leather too. The denim vest with its cut off sleeves flying his patches and designation in the club, was now replaced with the leather vest newer clubs called their cut. Her father had been one like Charlie, old school and ready to ride. No matter how fucked up they were at the time.
    She ignored them until she finished with Clem, and told her to give the rough looking sexy bastards at the end of the bar a message from her in five minutes. "Tell them to be ready to ride, I'll be waiting in the parking lot."
    She hated the idea of going back, but every time she'd tried to fight her visions, or ignored their warnings, she had paid dearly. This time she planned to embrace them. The plus side to all this was she could finally put paid to the old nightmares and hopefully some of the pain of her past. She was twenty-seven years old now, and felt as if she'd lived a lifetime already, and was working on life number two. Her sleepless night proved to her that she had no other options but to deal with it now.

She went into the back room and hefted her kit onto her Heritage. The one thing she'd taken with her when she left the hospital, and she would not give it up to ride bitch on another bike for the long trek home. She opened the double doors that faced the parking lot and rolled the bike out before closing the doors and listening for them to lock. She patted the tank and didn't feel in the least bit silly talking to it. "Hey, baby, are you ready to go home? Don't get too happy on the road, we will be back here soon and you will still be as beautiful as the day I bought you." She kicked the starter and revved the motor for a few moments making sure she was firing right, and drove around the backside of her building. The men were just coming out of the door and saw her waiting by their bikes.

Crazy Charlie saw her, stopped in his tracks for a moment, and started laughing. He held his sides, and finally sobered up enough to walk over to her, with the others a few steps behind him.

"I got it now, that black and pussy pink Hog, I remember when you got that one. We thought someone stole it or sold it when you didn't come back with the others. Old Merlin was a fucking wreck, and Muffy refused to believe you were dead. I just figured it out, Future, Oracle, and even the name of this place." He leaned in and clasped his hand onto her shoulder. "Well met, little witch. I can just see old Dorsey's face when he finds out you lived. He's gonna be lucky if someone don't kill him. He came back looking like he'd been slapped by his bitch, when the rest of us looked like we'd been beaten by the schoolyard bully. He told us that you died when one of Lucifer's Breed ran you over. He saw it happen. I got my head scrambled and we lost four people that night. You were one of them. You and Frenchy were the only ones we couldn't account for."

He looked back at the two men he was with and back to her. "After that night we patched over the Chiefs. That's how we got these two and about fifty others. Things have changed since then. You're going to be real surprised when you see what's happened."

She couldn't talk, if she tried, she knew she would bawl like a baby after its momma's teat. She locked arms with Charlie and nodded. She knew the two handsome men wanted an explanation, but she didn't owe them one fucking thing, and until she wanted to talk about it, they could get their information from Charlie. She didn't wait for them, they knew which way home was, and she left them standing on the blacktop as she drove away. It felt good to be going on a run again after the past years of only taking the bike out at night to blow the carbon out of her pipes. The Heritage had rear suspension and it rode like a dream. As soon as she hit the highway, she opened her up and stayed on it until she had to find an exit to get gas and use the bathroom. After filling the tank and grabbing a candy bar and a slushie, she strolled around the parking lot while she finished her snack, and it was back on the road for her.

Demon and Knight were both pissed when they heard Charlie's explanation. "Are you fuckin' kidding me? Why didn't they say this Oracle was a woman? And what does she have to do with that asshole Dorsey?"

"Dorsey swore to the whole club that she was dead. He saw her buy it. You two know we don't leave our dead if we can get them out. He made some big story about trying to get to her but there were too many of them for him to try, and she was dead anyway, so he couldn't save her, he saved himself. I hope Big Dog hasn't told anybody that you found her yet, 'cause if he has, Dorsey will be looking to get to her before she shows up at the crib.

"As for the bike, that flashy bitch sat outside the clubhouse for almost a month. It was gone one night and no one knew what happened to it the next day. I should have recognized her when we walked into this place, but you know my wings are not as strong as they used to be, especially after that night she went missing. She warned us, but that fucker Dorsey cut through what she was saying and challenged us all, calling us pussies and shit." He kept talking while Knight called Big Dog.

"It's too late, Dorsey is nowhere to be found, and he was at the club when you called in earlier, so he knows we found her. Dog has Poppa and Butch looking for him. I'm no Oracle, but my money says he'll either try to discredit her to the club as a rabbit. Or do his damndest to make sure she doesn't get there to talk. He's got a lot to lose if she can prove he lied. Hell, her being alive is proof that he lied."

Printed in Great Britain
by Amazon.co.uk, Ltd.,
Marston Gate.